He gazed at her in the cool blue twilight.

"You don't live out at your dad's ranch these days?"

"Um...no. I have a place in Bisons Creek, the top floor of the old Curry house. Remember it?"

"Sure. I'm just surprised, that's all. I thought you'd be living at home."

"No, Ford. I grew up and moved out."

His jaw tightened. "Sorry. I didn't mean to make you mad."

"Like you are?"

He held his hands out from his sides. "I'm not mad."

"You're clearly not happy to be showing me around. I was going to apologize, but that'll take more of your valuable time." She jolted down the steps and stalked past him.

"Caroline, wait. Caroline!" Ford caught up with her, grabbed her arm and pulled her around to face him. "Don't run away."

Breathing hard, she glared at him. "I am not running away. I'm trying to give you the distance you so obviously want." She hated that saying it hurt enough to sting her eyes with tears. "Let. Me. Go." She jerked her arm, trying to get free.

His fingers didn't loosen around her wrist. "I'm not letting go, so calm down. It's like fighting with a butterfly."

She stopped, appalled. "I am not a butterfly."

"No, you're a really beautiful woman who's driving me crazy."

Her jaw dropped open swallowed hard. "What

Dear Reader,

One of the best parts of writing fiction is being able to create the setting for your characters. You can put them into a world of glitz and glamour or, as I prefer, into a small town at the foot of Wyoming's Big Horn Mountains. You can make them cowboys with horses to ride and cattle to herd and a ranch to take care of spread out under the wide blue sky of the high plains. You can write about the importance of family and friends, community and faith, commitment and integrity. And there's nothing sexier than a man in jeans, boots and a cowboy hat.

Take the Marshall brothers—four cowboys bound by their ties to each other and to the land. There's trouble on the Circle M Ranch this summer and it will take all of them, working together, to handle it. Ford's story unfolds in *A Wife in Wyoming*, as he reconnects with the hometown girl he never forgot. He wasn't good enough for Caroline Donnelly in the old days, but he's changed. And so, it turns out, has she. Will those changes bring them closer together, or push them further apart?

I hope you enjoy getting to know the Marshalls and their world. I love to hear from readers—please feel free to send a note to PO Box 204, Vass, NC 28394, or contact me through my website, lynnettekentbooks.com.

As ever,

Lynnette Kent

A WIFE IN WYOMING

LYNNETTE KENT

HARLEQUIN® AMERICAN ROMANCE®

Recycling programs
for this product may
not exist in your area.

ISBN-13: 978-0-373-75565-3

A Wife in Wyoming

Copyright © 2015 by Cheryl B. Bacon

Printed in U.S.A.

Lynnette Kent lives on a farm in southeastern North Carolina with her six horses and six dogs. When she isn't busy riding, driving or feeding animals, she loves to tend her gardens and read and write books.

Books by Lynnette Kent

HARLEQUIN AMERICAN ROMANCE

Christmas at Blue Moon Ranch
Smoky Mountain Reunion
Smoky Mountain Home
A Holiday to Remember
Jesse: Merry Christmas, Cowboy
A Convenient Proposal

HARLEQUIN SUPERROMACE

The Last Honest Man
The Fake Husband
Single with Kids
Abby's Christmas
The Prodigal Texan

Visit the Author Profile page
at Harlequin.com for more titles

Chapter One

There was trouble on the Circle M Ranch, and Ford Marshall had come to take care of it. His brothers were doing their best, but when problems arose, the four Marshall boys handled them together. Always had, always would.

Ford had driven more than a thousand miles in the past two days, with only the last fifty left to go. Still, he pulled over at the top of the final descent, got out of the truck and went to stand on the edge of a five-hundred-foot drop. He stared down at the Powder River Valley laid out below, where the slopes of the Big Horn Mountains gave way to rolling, grass-covered plains. The landscape was as familiar to him as the palm of his hand, and just as vital.

How long, Ford wondered, since he'd enjoyed this view?

Fifteen years, probably— the summer after high school graduation, when he'd helped herd cattle down to lower pasture before heading off to college. He'd returned to visit since, but not at this time of year. Summer jobs, classes, internships, law school…he'd been busy then, and he'd been even busier since he'd joined one of the biggest firms in San Francisco and started working his way up.

For now, though, he was home—not forever, not even for the whole summer. But with time enough to stand here as the sun set behind him, tinting the valley blue and purple. Time enough to pull the fresh air into his lungs and listen to the evening breeze rustle through the pines.

Time. The one commodity he didn't have in his portfolio these days.

Ford headed back to the truck, started the engine and eased onto the empty highway, heading downhill. His law partners weren't happy about the leave of absence. His clients... Hell, his clients were furious. He'd jeopardized his career—plus the security and status it provided—to take these weeks off.

But family came first. And so he coasted down from the mountains and breezed south out of Buffalo toward their little town of Bisons Creek, where he headed up the county road to the one place that he still, after all these years away, called home.

AT THE HOUSE the screened front door stood wide open to the night air. Ford crossed the porch and stepped into the dark living room. "Anybody home?"

A *woof!* and the scrabble of dog claws on the plank floor announced the approach of Honey, the chubby golden retriever who'd been the ranch's top dog for the past ten years.

"Hey there, Honey Bear." He bent to ruffle her ears and scratch her along her spine as she circled in front of him, panting with delight. "Yeah, you're a good girl, aren't you?"

Boot heels thudded down the hall from the rear of the house. "It's about time you showed up." His brother Garrett gave him a fake slug to the jaw before closing him into a bear hug. "We've got a million questions about this insurance stuff that nobody will answer. How was your drive?"

"Fine." Ford drew back and lifted an eyebrow. "Where's the boss?"

Garrett tilted his head in the direction of the bedrooms. "Sulky as a bear. I'd go in with a rifle, if I were you."

"When's dinner?"

"When you make it."

"Just like the old days." Ford had started cooking for their motherless family when he was ten. "Let me talk to Wyatt first. And can we turn on some lights in this house?"

"Leave it to you to get us organized." Garrett flipped a switch and the living room became visible. Welcoming.

"That's better." As Ford started toward his older brother's room, Honey slipped ahead of him to lead the way. The lights were off at the far end of the hall, which was strange so early in the evening. Who the hell was running this place?

He reached for a lamp just inside the bedroom door and switched it on. "Hey, Boss. No self-respecting rancher is asleep at 8:00 p.m."

"No self-respecting rancher gets thrown from a horse, lands on his butt and breaks his damn back." Wyatt put up a hand from where he lay flat in bed. "Welcome home."

His brother's hearty grip allowed Ford to relax a little. "Thanks."

But Wyatt was frowning. "You didn't have to leave your job, though. Garrett and Dylan are managing okay."

"Yeah, right," Garrett said from the door. "The two of us finish about half of what you did on your own in a single day. No problems there."

"The work'll get done."

"It will get done faster with more hands to help."

There was an edge to his brother's tone, and Ford gathered they'd had this argument before. "We'll manage the chores, one way or the other. Right now I'm more interested in food. What do you feel like, Wyatt?"

"I'm not hungry." He'd turned his face toward the TV flickering in the corner.

"You're always hungry."

"Not when I spend the whole damn day in bed." A metal brace was sprawled across the dresser, conspicuously unused.

"Okay. I'll figure it out and bring you a plate."

"Don't bother."

In the kitchen Ford raised an eyebrow as he met Garrett's eyes. "How long has he been this way?"

"Ten days since he came home from the hospital. Won't take the pain pills they gave him, just lies there except when he has to pee."

"I should have been here sooner." He moved toward the refrigerator. "You should have called right away."

"I didn't know the injury would get him so down."

Ford pulled four T-bone steaks out of the freezer and headed for the oven. "He won't use the brace?"

"I can't convince him to put it on. I guess he's planning to lie in bed until he stops hurting."

"Not a chance. We'll get him on his feet. Right now find me some potatoes."

In thirty minutes he'd prepared four steak dinners, the task as familiar as if he still did it every night, instead of twice a year. He debated cutting Wyatt's meat up, but decided he didn't want the food thrown at him.

He returned to his brother's room. "Dinner's ready."

"I said I'm not hungry." But Wyatt's stomach betrayed him, gurgling loud enough to be heard outside the house.

Ford laughed. "I know the truth when I hear it. Come out and eat at the table like a man."

His older brother glared at him from under lowered brows. "You're making trouble."

"You're being a pain in the butt."

Wyatt swore, loudly, but he rolled to the side of the bed

and then off, landing carefully on his knees. Pushing up with his hands, he straightened his legs before he could finally lever his top half upright.

Ford picked up the metal brace. "That's quite a process."

Wyatt muttered something unintelligible and presented his back. With a few fumbles, Ford got the brace over his brother's head and settled it on his shoulders with the straps fastened tight.

"There ya go."

At that moment the screen door in the front of the house slammed. "Got some food somewhere?" Dylan called. "I'm starving."

As Wyatt walked stiffly into the bright kitchen light, the youngest Marshall gave a whistle. "Look at you, Boss. We'll have you in the saddle in no time." He walked toward Ford. "So you finally came home. I've got a horse with your saddle on it out in the corral." Then he came in for a hug. "Welcome back," he said in a low voice, which Ford understood meant *we need you*.

"Yep," Ford said, meaning *I'll take care of everything*. He slapped Dylan on the shoulder. "Let's eat."

For a while the only sounds were chewing and swallowing as the four of them dug into their steaks. Ford took the opportunity to study each of his brothers, assessing changes since his last visit. Dylan, with his dark brown hair worn a little long and a sensitive curve to his mouth just like their mother's, still looked young enough to be in college, though he'd graduated five years ago. Garrett's hair was a lighter brown and neatly styled, probably to please his church congregation. Right now his blue eyes were shadowed and a little strained—he'd always been the worrier. Wyatt shared Dylan's brown eyes and Garrett's hair, cut in the practical, no-fuss way he'd worn for years. Age never told on Wyatt's face; he looked pretty much the same at thirty-four as he had at twenty-four... except tired this time. Was it his injury, or was something else going on?

Ford would find out sooner or later. No need to push the issue. "So what's the plan for tomorrow?" he asked instead, which brought to order the usual dinner table board meeting for Marshall Brothers, Incorporated. Details for moving cattle, fences to be checked and machinery to get tuned up came under review, as always.

Only Wyatt hardly said a word.

"So what do you think, Boss?" Ford pushed his empty plate away and looked at his brother.

Wyatt glanced up from his plate. "What do I think about what?"

"We decided we'd flood the eastside pastures, grow our own brand of Wyoming rice."

The oldest Marshall set down his fork and knife with a clank. "That's the stupidest idea I ever heard of. Rice won't grow..." He noticed the grin on Ford's face and frowned. "What's your point?"

"That you're not listening. Or eating much."

"I'm not *doing* much. No reason to eat."

The preacher in the family propped his elbows on the table. "Can't you view this as a vacation? You're always saying you don't get a chance to read. When did you last take a day off?"

Ford answered the question. "When he was fourteen, maybe. Before Dad died."

Garrett nodded. "Twenty years without a break?"

Wyatt shook his head. "I get plenty of downtime. I don't need a vacation. I need to get back to work."

Dylan clucked his tongue. "Well, that's not happening in the immediate future. The doctor wants you quiet for at least three months." He leaned his chair back, balancing on the two rear legs. "And since you're staying still for a change, I want to do some sketches, work up plans for a life-size carving of your head. I found a piece of petrified pine that would be perfect."

Wyatt's frown evolved into an expression of horror. "I don't want a statue of me sitting around somewhere for people to stare at. Next thing I know, you'll be exhibiting me in one of your art shows. Keep your chair on the floor."

The chair clattered as Dylan straightened up. "Thanks for the vote of confidence. I suppose you'd also suggest I spend less time carving and more time doing meaningful work?"

"As a matter of fact, I might."

Cheeks flushed, brown eyes blazing, Dylan got to his feet. "Well, as a matter of fact, I might tell you to go to hell."

Ford rolled his eyes. "Dylan—"

But the youngest Marshall stomped out of the room without listening. The slap of the screen door announced that he'd left the house. And he'd broken one of the cardinal rules—leaving his plate on the table for someone else to carry to the kitchen.

Wyatt passed a hand over his face. "I can't seem to say the right thing to him anymore."

Ford stacked Dylan's plate on top of his own. "Would a statue be so bad?"

Wyatt glared at him from under lowered brows. "Why don't *you* model for him?"

"Maybe I will." Ford struck a pose with the dishes balanced on one hand. "You could stand it in the corner and tip your hat every time you walk by me. We'll put a plaque on the pedestal—Ford Marshall, Renowned Attorney."

"That'll be the day." Garrett walked around to pick up Wyatt's plate. "We're more likely to turn your face to the wall and aim a swift kick at your butt when you're not here to help out."

Ford led the way into the kitchen. "Spoken like a true man of the cloth. I thought ministers were supposed to be kind and gentle with their flocks."

"Brothers are exempted from that rule. Besides, I'll bet you haven't been to church since you were last here. Am I wrong?"

"Just can't find a preacher in San Francisco as good as you."

"Right. I believe that one. Well, plan on getting up tomorrow morning and heading into town, because around here the Marshalls still show up in the pew on Sunday morning."

"Yes, sir."

Garrett took the dishcloth out of Ford's hand. "You cooked. I'll clean up. Go talk to the boss. Maybe get him outside for a few minutes."

"Right."

He found Wyatt where they'd left him, sitting alone in the dining room, staring at his bottle of beer. "Want to take a walk? It's a pretty night."

"I was thinking about going to bed."

"Me, too. But I want to stretch my legs first. Come on." He took hold of the chair and pulled it away as Wyatt stood up.

A sound very close to a growl came from Wyatt's throat. "I can manage my own damn chair."

"I'm sure you can. Want me to shove it into the backs of your knees? Then we could have a wrestling match, like we used to, and you could beat the snot out of me, like you used to. Would that make you feel better?"

Wyatt snorted a laugh. "Probably."

"Not me, though." They walked through the house, out the front door and down the three porch steps, with Ford pretending that he wasn't on guard in case something happened, and Wyatt pretending he didn't realize what Ford was doing. Out in the open, they both took a deep breath.

"I swear my lungs can't fill up all the way when I'm in the city," Ford said. "The air's just too thick, too heavy."

"I know what you mean." Wyatt lifted his face as far as the brace permitted. "The mountains, the grasslands… the pure space of it all gives a man enough room to stretch out and live. I'm surprised, that you stay in the city as long as you do."

"That's where the work is. Not many prospects for a high-powered law practice in Bisons Creek."

"Guess not. Wyoming's got its share of corporate lawyers these days, though, what with the oil and coal companies all over the place. And we never run out of bad guys looking for a defense lawyer. Never stop needing prosecutors to punish them, either."

"Of course not." Ford stared up at the Wyoming stars, the familiar constellations in their early-summer formations, twinkling like far-off candles against the black velvet sky. "I'll keep it in mind, if I decide to shift gears." He let a silence fill with the sounds of nearby crickets and the whisper of the wind. "Everything going all right on the Circle M?"

The boss didn't answer right away. "With ranching, there's always something going wrong," he said at last. "Cattle prices are down, the grass-fed market demand is slow. Winter lasted longer than usual, so we're late moving herds into the higher pastures. The Forest Service has limited the parcels we can use, which means fattening up these early steers is gonna be harder." He blew a rueful snort. "Same stuff, different day."

"Well, my investments are sound, the dividends are high and we've got a solid buffer in place. If you have cash flow problems, just let me know."

"Sure." Wyatt's hand came to rest on his shoulder.

"Mostly, we're just glad to have you here, Ford. Thanks for making the effort."

"The Marshalls stick together," Ford told him, meeting his brother's dark gaze with his own. "I wouldn't be anywhere else."

FROM HER PLACE in the church choir, Caroline Donnelly noticed the new arrival as soon as he entered the building on Sunday morning. He was tall and broad-shouldered like all the Marshall brothers, but Ford was the one blond in the bunch, his hair still the bright, sleek gold color he'd inherited from his dad.

Mr. Marshall had been her father's business manager as far back as Caroline could remember. She'd known him as the smiling man who kept a bowl of hard candy on his desk and always let her have a piece when she came by.

"Sweets for the sweet," he would say and wink at her.

The Marshall boys had never come with their dad to the Donnelly ranch—her dad had strict rules about who she could play with—but she'd gone to school with the oldest three. Because he was five years behind her, she hadn't seen much of Dylan, but there was always talk in town about the latest stunt the youngest Marshall had pulled.

Ford, however, hadn't been one for pulling stunts. Even before they lost their parents, he'd been the serious Marshall, the driven, studious one. He seemed the same now, with his expensive haircut and his designer jacket worn over a pair of jeans.

Actually, he looked even better now—like every woman's fantasy of a cleaned-up cowboy with lots of money. It was all pretty much make-believe, but oh, so nice to dream about. His successful law career was a claim to fame as far as the citizens of Bisons Creek were concerned.

"Psst. Caroline!" Beth Forbes, the woman next to her, tugged on her sleeve. "Time to start!"

Caroline stood up belatedly and opened her choir book. Thank goodness she knew the opening song by heart, since she was on the wrong page. Those Marshall boys had always distracted her from what she was supposed to be doing. Especially Ford.

She tried to concentrate during the service, but she found her gaze straying to his face too often for her own comfort. They'd been in the same grade and some of the same courses—English, history, math. He hadn't grabbed attention by clowning around or disrupting class, the way other boys did. But none of the troublemakers bothered him or tried to goad him into acting out. Something about Ford kept everybody at a distance.

Listening with half an ear to Garrett's sermon, Caroline recalled the day Ford had returned to school after his dad died. Mr. Marshall hadn't worked at the Donnelly ranch for a couple of years by then, but she'd wanted to say something since he'd been a big part of her life. So she'd stopped at Ford's locker just before lunch.

"I'm sorry about your dad," she'd said, meaning every word. "He was kind to me when I was little."

Ford had slammed his locker shut, making her jump. He'd turned in her direction, but his dark blue eyes looked right through her. After a moment, he nodded and then walked away.

She'd been too spooked to speak to him again.

Not today, though. Today she would talk to him and make sure he listened, because what she had to say was important. Not just to her—though the work she was trying to do had cost her dearly—but to the whole community of Bisons Creek.

Butterflies flitted around in her stomach as she thought about talking with Ford. She'd been nervous enough when she'd expected to have to consult with Wyatt, but Garrett had told her that Ford was running the ranch this summer and that he was the one she'd have to convince. At least she'd have Garrett to back her up. Ford couldn't walk away from the two of them.

She hoped.

As usual, Dylan fell asleep during his brother's sermon, but today Ford elbowed him awake for the final hymn. In the choir room afterward, Caroline shelved her folder and spent a minute at the mirror to add a swipe of lipstick to her mouth and make sure her hair was okay. She put a hand on her stomach and drew a deep breath—the butterflies had taken up kickboxing.

Finally she went to the social hall, where refreshments were provided, giving members a chance to greet each other and chat over cookies and lemonade or coffee. Garrett had promised that he would make sure Ford stayed.

And there he was, surrounded by folks who hadn't seen him since the last time he was home at Christmas, all of them asking about his glamorous San Francisco law practice and how Wyatt was doing. Dylan hosted his own fan club, composed of the single women from eighteen to thirty who wanted to be flirted with. The youngest Marshall was only too happy to oblige.

Caroline wolfed down three sugar cookies and a glass of lemonade before the crowd thinned enough that she stood a chance of getting through. As soon as she stepped into the circle, Ford glanced her way. His eyes narrowed slightly before refocusing on the face of the person talking to him. He smiled at the woman—such a nice smile, but one he used so rarely. And never with her.

If it were up to me, Caroline thought, *I'd make him laugh at least three times a day.*

Maybe, if the project she wanted his help on got going, she might get the chance!

Finally, with most of the congregation out of the

way, she moved close enough to say, "Hello, Ford." She breathed deep and held out her hand. "Welcome home."

For a second—just an instant—he hesitated. Then his hand took hers, and his eyes brightened. "Hello there, Caroline. Good to see you. It's been a long time."

The warmth of his skin against hers was nearly as distracting as the smile. "Fifteen years, believe it or not, since graduation. I hear you've done magnificent things in San Francisco."

"I do my job. What have you been up to?"

Garrett stepped up beside his brother. "Caroline runs the Department of Family Services in Bisons Creek. She's working with the area's disadvantaged families."

"Really?" Ford lifted a disbelieving eyebrow.

Caroline nodded. "Really," she said, and at that moment realized they were still holding hands. She slid hers quickly out of his grasp. "I majored in psychology, got my master's degree in social work and was with the department in Casper for four years before moving back here. There are people in trouble in this area, just like anywhere else, especially the teenagers. High school is a lot more dangerous now than when we were there."

He crossed his arms over his chest, which only made his shoulders broader. "So I understand. Garrett said you have a project you want to talk to me about."

"I do." She glanced around and noticed the volunteers were cleaning up the refreshment table. "Now might not be the best time, though. Could you meet me in town for lunch tomorrow?"

He glanced at Garrett. "I'm here to take on some of the work Wyatt can't get to. I expect I'll be in the saddle all day tomorrow. What about right now? Kate's Café is still open on Sundays, right?"

"I've got some sick parishioners to visit," Garrett said. "I can't take a break for lunch today."

Caroline hesitated. She'd expected to have Garrett's support when she explained her plan. Would she be as persuasive by herself?

Ford read her indecision. "If you're busy, maybe later in the week…?"

"No, not at all." She would do this and do it well, for the kids. "Right now is perfect. Shall we meet there in about ten minutes?"

Dylan sauntered up. "Hey, Miss Caroline. You are looking especially fine today."

She gave him the big smile he deserved. "Thank you so much, sleepyhead."

He flushed and pushed his dark hair back off his face. "Stayed up till dawn working on a piece. Then somebody stomps in at seven and drags me out of bed to feed horses." His gaze went to Ford. "So I'm a little short on shut-eye." He yawned for emphasis. "Going home to bed."

Ford propped his hands on his hips. "That leaves me without a ride."

Caroline swallowed hard. "No problem. We can go to the café in my truck. I'll run you home after."

His gaze, meeting hers, was hard to read. "Great. I'm interested to hear what you have to say." He stepped forward and pressed the tips of his fingers against her shoulder blade. "Shall we?"

They got a few interested stares from lingering church members as she led the way to her truck. Caroline wanted to yell, "Just business!" at them but restrained herself. She wondered if Ford would prefer that she had.

She unlocked the truck from a distance with the electronic key and was surprised when he followed her to the driver's side to open the door.

"Th-thanks," she said, after climbing in with as much grace as she could manage in a dress.

"You're welcome." He shut the door, came around the

back and swung into the passenger seat with a cowboy's smooth control.

"You're still at home in a truck, I see." She let her gaze brush over him as she turned her head to reverse out of the parking space. "Do you drive one in San Francisco?"

"I've got a Mercedes for town. The clients prefer it."

"Do they know your ranch background at the law office?"

"My partners are aware. I have some pictures in my office, but most people don't notice. They're concerned with their own issues, not mine."

"Not like Bisons Creek, where everybody wants to hear your business?"

"Not remotely like Bisons Creek, which has its good and bad points."

The drive to Kate's Café took all of three minutes. Caroline parked in a spot the next block up—one of the five blocks that made up Main Street—because the lot around the restaurant was full. They didn't talk as they walked to the café, but the never-ending Wyoming wind blew her hair in all directions.

Caroline sighed. She would be giving an important presentation to the most intelligent, educated and sophisticated man she knew in front of at least half of the town's citizens, and she'd look as if she'd walked through a tornado. Great.

Ford held the door open for her again when they reached the café. The bell on the handle rang as he came through behind her, and every face in the building turned in their direction. Caroline kept her smile in place and scanned the suddenly silent crowd for a table.

"Here ya go, son." Marvin Harris stood up from the table in the front corner. "The missus and I are done. You're welcome to sit here."

"Thanks, Mr. Harris." Ford shook the older man's hand

and his wife's. "Good to see you, Mrs. Harris. How are those grandsons of yours? I hear they're real firecrackers."

"You got that right." Mr. Harris chuckled and rubbed his hands together. "Caught them one day trying to fly out of the hay loft with a pair of wings they'd made out of cardboard. Lucky they didn't break their darn fool necks!" He turned to Caroline. "Hello, Missy. How's your mama these days?"

"Just fine, Mr. Harris, thank you." At least, she hoped so. She hadn't visited with her mom in almost a month.

Mrs. Harris walked up to Ford and patted his arm. "It's about time you finished with this San Francisco foolishness, boy, and came back home where you belong. Get yourself a wife and some kids and settle down." As she left, she gave Caroline a wink that Ford would surely notice. "You two have a nice afternoon."

Just kill me now, Caroline said to herself. *It can only get worse from here.*

Chapter Two

By the time Ford had pulled out Caroline's chair and then settled into his own, one of the waitresses had come to clean the table. "Thanks, Angie."

Caroline said the same thing at the same moment. Their gazes met and held before sliding apart.

"How's school?" Ford asked the waitress.

"Good." The college sophomore gave him a grin. "I made the rodeo team. Cool, huh?"

He nodded. "As long as you remember to study for classes."

Angie stuck her tongue out at him and turned to Caroline. "You rode for the University of Wyoming team, didn't you, Caroline?"

Caroline brushed her hair behind her shoulders. "For three years. I dropped out my senior year—too busy."

The waitress sighed. "I'll never be too busy for rodeo. I'm hoping to go pro when I graduate." She loaded up plates and glasses on one arm. "What can I get you two to drink?"

Caroline asked for water, Ford ordered a soda and Angie went on her way, which left them facing each other across the table. "Glad to be back in town?" Caroline asked him.

He gave a rueful smile. "Something of a challenge, I

admit. The locals are ready to plan your life out for you, aren't they?"

"Oh, yes. Not to mention telling you exactly what you did wrong in the past."

"But surely you don't hear that often. You were everybody's favorite rodeo queen."

She rolled her eyes and frowned. "Hardly."

"Oh, definitely. That's how I remember you—prom queen, homecoming queen, rodeo queen." Her expression didn't lighten. "You won all the votes, every time." For good reason, since she'd been the prettiest girl in the school.

Not to mention the daughter of one of the richest ranchers in Johnson County. "Is your mother doing well? Your brother still riding bulls?" He wouldn't bring up her dad. They were likely to have very different perspectives on George Donnelly.

She met his gaze, and he was surprised to see sadness in her eyes. "I haven't talked to Reid for…a while. My mom says he's doing okay, but will be retiring from the rodeo pretty soon to come back and work on the ranch with Daddy."

"That'll be…interesting." As much as he enjoyed working with his own family, Ford didn't envy Caroline's brother a life with his father as his boss. His own dad had spent ten faithful years working at the Donnelly ranch and, from what Ford remembered, George Donnelly had been a tough taskmaster.

He also remembered how, just months after his mom's death, Donnelly had fired his dad without a second thought. The resulting downward spiral had cost him and his brothers their remaining parent. Though Donnelly couldn't logically be held responsible for his dad becoming an alcoholic and killing himself in a car accident two years later, his indifference certainly hadn't improved the situation.

But the Marshall boys had turned out just fine without anybody's help. Wyatt's strong hand and determination had seen them through. In the end, the only people you could rely on were your family.

"Working with my dad is a challenge," Caroline said, in an unexpected echo of Ford's thoughts. "I'm not sure Reid will stick it out. He can be pretty volatile himself."

Angie reappeared with their drinks. "What can I get y'all to eat? Chicken fried steak is the special today," she announced. "Comes with mashed potatoes, green beans and Kate's homemade rolls."

"Sounds great," he and Caroline said in unison. Again.

"That'll be two." Angie wrote on her notepad. "Back in a bit."

When Ford looked over at Caroline, she had set her forearms on the edge of the table and leaned a little toward him. He gathered they were about to get down to business.

"We're here," she started, "because I want to tell you what I'm planning. This is a project Garrett and I are very excited about, and I think the Circle M Ranch would be the perfect setting to use." Her expressive face wore the prize-winning smile he'd never forgotten.

Ford drew a breath and relaxed into his chair. "Okay, I'm ready. Go for it."

She talked without stopping for at least fifteen minutes while Angie delivered their plates and refilled his drink, while he ate and Caroline took a bite here and there. Ford listened and didn't interrupt—she was clearly in the moment and very prepared with numbers and details, genuinely committed to her plan. Only when she actually finished and sat silent for almost a minute did he try to get a word in edgewise.

"You've worked hard on this."

She nodded, chewing a bite of her steak.

"And you're really driven to succeed with it."

Another even more vigorous nod of her head.

"So let me go over what I've understood from your presentation. You want to start up a summer program for at-risk teenagers—the ones who have gotten into trouble at school, or with the law, or who have problems at home, like documented abuse. Not hardened criminals, but kids who still could be rescued and sent in a different, safer direction."

"That's right." She took a sip of water. "I've screened all the children I work with very carefully to identify the right kids for the group. I don't want to put anybody at risk. I just want to give them a different experience, a chance to see that they can succeed in life."

"Right. And the kids in your program will reside at the Circle M, where they would be expected to learn how to do ranch work—riding, herding, roping, feeding, treating…whatever is on the schedule for me and my brothers to do, the kids would also do."

"Yes. I know they would have a learning curve—none of them have a ranching background."

"So they would have to learn how to ride, and ride pretty well. They'd have only a couple of weeks to acquire the kind of skills it takes a ranch hand several years to master."

"You would be doing the main part of the work, but you'd be doing it anyway, so it's not a loss for you."

"As long as they didn't do anything dumb and hurt themselves."

"Well—"

"But you're expecting us to be there to protect them and see that they don't get injured, along with doing our own work."

"I know it's asking something extra, but I'll be there,

too, so I could do a lot of the supervision and help out—I was a pretty good roper in my day."

"Sure. And you were a champion rider. I get that. What about the legal liabilities? Will the parents sign a waiver and a consent form, just in case something does happen?"

"People stay at working guest ranches all the time, Ford. They agree to hold the owner and the ranch workers blameless in case of injuries or…or death…if something happens. We would cover the Circle M and the Marshalls the same way. The parents would agree to it. And we'd have a medical consent form in case we needed care fast."

"There is no fast medical care in Bisons Creek."

"Ah, but there you're wrong. We have a doctor coming to town this summer, and she'll be opening her own clinic. If something happened, we'd be just a few minutes away."

"Progress is wonderful," he said drily. "So these kids, who aren't the most upstanding citizens, are going to live and work at the ranch for three months, with access to our animals, our equipment, tools and house. We're supposed to trust they won't do any damage or take anything. We have computers, you know. Cell phones. TVs and radios and audio equipment. There's beer in the fridge, whiskey in the sideboard. But you believe your kids will be immune to the temptations."

Caroline was quiet for a moment, staring down at the table in front of her. Then she looked up at him. "I have to be honest—three of the boys were caught stealing candy from a gas station a few weeks ago. The manager took them to court, for their own good, he said."

Ford sat up straight in his chair. "And you want to bring them into our home?"

"They're boys, Ford. Little more than children. The judge was going to sentence them to community service all summer, but I persuaded her to let me try this program. I want to show these kids where choosing the right side can take you. I think they will be immune because bad behavior will carry penalties."

"What kind of penalties?"

"If they fail this program, they return to the court system and end up with a juvenile record. They don't deserve that. They're not bad. Just confused."

He blew out a deep breath, just as Angie sidled up to their table. "Dessert?"

Caroline shook her head. "I couldn't possibly."

But Ford nodded. "Kate's apple pie? With ice cream?"

"Coming up."

He'd welcomed the interruption, though it only delayed the inevitable. He wasn't a man who went around kicking puppies. But right now he felt like one.

Propping his elbows on the table, he captured Caroline's gaze with his. "Listen, I appreciate what you're trying to do. I served several internships in family law, dealing with these kinds of kids. I mentored them. I wrote briefs for their court appearances. I investigated their home lives, their schools, their friends. Do you know what I saw?"

"What?"

"Nine out of ten didn't give a damn about what we were doing for them. And the ones who did couldn't escape, even if they wanted to. I don't think I caused meaningful change for a single kid I worked with."

Caroline clasped her hands together on the table. "That's terribly sad. But does it mean you stop trying?"

He wasn't getting through to her. "Why are you so determined to implement this plan? What do you hope to gain?"

Her chin lifted, and a stubborn light came into her eyes. "Why are you so opposed to it?"

Ford shook his head. "You first."

She blew out a short breath. "I honestly believe that everybody deserves a chance to succeed, regardless of their income, their family situation, their history. Kids in particular ought to be offered options for a better life. What I hope to gain is a better place to live for all of us."

"So you're basically trying to save the world?" He meant it as a joke, to ease the tension.

Caroline didn't smile. "Somebody needs to. Why not me…and the Marshall brothers?"

"Because some people can't be saved." Ford folded his arms across his chest. "No matter what you do for them, they break the rules out of self-interest and simple, down-right meanness. In the process, they often hurt the people around them, including the ones trying to help them."

"These are kids, Ford. They're not old enough for meanness."

"This is my family, Caroline. This is our home, which I spend my life working to protect. You may believe a signature on a release form reduces our liability. As an attorney, I can tell you that lawsuits are easy to file and hard to evade. An injured kid could cost us thousands, even hundreds of thousands of dollars, maybe cost us the ranch itself. More important, our reputations are vulnerable in this situation. One of those kids could claim they were molested on the ranch, and all of us would become suspect. Frankly, I've come too far in my professional and personal life to take that risk lightly. My brothers are good men—I would hate for them to deal with that kind of public harassment. You wouldn't be immune, either. Your job—your whole life—could be ruined because of a teenager's whim."

She didn't flinch. "I think it's worth taking the chance."

"I disagree."

"You're saying no." Her face was pale, her big eyes wider than ever and, as he watched, they started to shine with unshed tears.

He let his arms relax, resting his fingertips on the table.

"I'm really sorry, Caroline. I understand what this means to you, what you hope it might mean to the kids. But I'm saying—"

Angie slid a saucer laden with pie and a huge scoop of ice cream across the table in front of him. "Jerk," she said before walking away.

He used his index finger to move the scoop of ice cream from the table back on top of the pie. "What I'm saying is that I'll vote no when the time comes."

Caroline frowned. "Vote?"

"That's how the Marshalls make decisions." Ford pushed the plate away. He'd lost his appetite. "Everybody gets a vote on something that affects the ranch as a whole. Like this program of yours."

"What do you do if there's a tie?"

"Wyatt's the boss, so he gets an extra vote if he wants one."

Hope replaced despair in Caroline's pretty face. "So even if your vote is against me, there's still a chance that the Marshalls as a family would agree?"

Ford sat forward, resting his arms on the table. "My vote isn't against you."

There wasn't anything about Caroline to vote against, that he could see. The tousled mahogany hair, the rosy cheeks and shining eyes, the way a lightweight yellow dress set off her curvy figure and slender legs… No, not a single thing to object to, in his opinion. "I don't consider your plan to be in our best interest. That's all."

"Wyatt may think differently. Garrett certainly does. What happens then?"

"I guess you go forward with your project."

"But you'd still oppose me?"

"If the family votes yes, I'll cooperate."

She shook her head. "Spoken like a lawyer. I'll just

have to hope that Wyatt and Dylan are willing to take a chance on my kids."

"We'll talk it over and let you know as soon as we've reached a decision."

She gave him a bright smile. "Then I guess the faster I get you home, the faster I'll hear the answer."

Which gave him a fair idea of where he stood as far as Caroline Donnelly was concerned.

THOUGH SHE'D GROWN UP practically next door to the Marshall brothers, Caroline had never been to the Circle M Ranch. Yet here she was on a Sunday afternoon, driving Ford Marshall home. He looked relaxed enough in the passenger seat, but he seemed to fill up the space around her, which made getting a decent breath difficult. When she tried, his scent teased her nose with hints of pine and grass edged with an exotic tang she couldn't name.

His silence was getting on her nerves, so she spoke the thought at the front of her mind. "You and your brothers didn't grow up at the Circle M, did you?"

"No." The hand lying on his thigh fisted and then relaxed. "My folks had a house in town. When Dad died—" he paused and drew a deep breath "—Wyatt went to work for Henry MacPherson at the ranch. After a couple of years, the old man had us move out here. Dylan was twelve, I think. I stayed for the summer before heading off to college."

"So you really haven't lived here that long." She turned off the road to drive between two stacked-rock columns, which supported an iron arch carrying the ranch's brand— a circle with an M inside. "You didn't come back for the summers, did you?"

He glanced in her direction, his eyebrows raised. "You kept track?"

Caroline felt her cheeks flush. "It's just...I mean, for

those first few years, the graduating class got together, you know, to have a party during the summer and find out what everybody was doing. But you were never there." Even that was admitting too much. Why had she noticed whether Ford Marshall came or not?

"As I said earlier, I worked most summers in legal offices, getting experience to put on my law school applications."

"But you probably wouldn't have come even if you were in town."

"Probably not. I wasn't Mr. Social Scene when I was here." After a moment, he continued. "But you were. I'm not surprised you made all the parties."

That was the third strike, as far as Caroline was concerned. She stomped on the brake, put the truck into Park and turned in the seat to face him. "What did I do to you that made you resent me so much?"

Again, that look of surprise. "What are you talking about?"

"That's the third time you've insinuated that I'm shallow and stupid."

"You said you got your master's degree. That's not stupid. I just meant you were Miss Popularity."

"There you go again. Yes, I was popular in high school. When did that become a crime?"

"This is a ridiculous argument for two adults to have. High school was fifteen years ago."

"But whatever grudge you've got against me is standing in the way of helping some troubled kids get the future they deserve. So I want to deal with it now and move on."

His hand fisted again. "I was a poor orphan kid from the wrong side of town. You were the rich socialite with the world and most people in it at your feet. I grew up being reminded I wasn't good enough to breathe the same air as George Donnelly's kids. But I'm over it. Can we drive now?"

Caroline continued to stare at him. His explanation fit the facts and yet…didn't. What wasn't he saying? "People do change, you know."

"Yes, they do. Some more than others." He opened the door and dropped to the ground. "Thanks for the ride. Garrett will call you after we have the family meeting." With a two-fingered salute from an imaginary hat brim, he set off in the direction of the house.

As he strode off, Caroline noticed the summertime beauty of the lush pastureland around her. Circle M Ranch sat at the base of the Big Horn Mountains, where a winter's worth of snow had brought up green grass and gorgeous wildflowers—pink fireweed, yellow buttercups, white daisies and blue lupines.

She also appreciated the physique of the man walking away from her. He'd taken off his jacket, and she enjoyed the play of shoulder muscles under his dark plaid shirt, the fit of denim over his narrow hips and long legs. He had certainly changed since high school—though still lean, he carried himself with a confidence the skinny teenager had lacked.

Yet he'd been the cutest boy in school. Which was why she'd always hugged to herself a secret crush on Ford Marshall.

Not that she would tell him about it. He was way too sure of himself for her to give him that kind of advantage. Maybe she'd had a lucky escape in high school—a man like Ford would dominate a woman's life rather than simply share it. And Caroline wouldn't surrender her hard-won independence just to be someone's "little woman."

This summer, though, she wanted him on her side, which meant mending fences. So she put the truck in gear and followed him down the road, slowing as she came alongside him. Through the open window, she called, "I'm sorry for being cranky. Get in and I'll take you the rest of the way."

He shook his head and kept walking. "That's okay. I don't get out enough in San Francisco. Feels good."

"Are you going to make me follow you all the way to the house?"

"It's only about a half mile."

"Come on, Ford. Get in."

He stopped, set his hands on his hips and stood facing away from her, gazing out over the land. They were on a bit of a rise and could see all the way to the mountains, plus the ranch buildings in between—a timber-sided house, a big red barn with corrals around it and other structures.

"It's beautiful," Caroline said. "I never realized what a view you have over the valley. My dad's ranch isn't nearly this pretty." Especially considering all the metal buildings set up to house his quarter horse breeding business. With the stallion barn, the mare barn and foaling barn, the indoor arena, offices and equipment sheds, not to mention the landing strip for his plane, the place resembled a military base more than a Wyoming ranch.

"Yeah, it's pretty special." He came to the door and leaned one arm on the windowsill. "You're a problem, Caroline Donnelly. Do you know that?"

"I don't intend to be. Why don't we let the past be over, and start from here and now?" She held her hand out across the seat between them. "Deal?"

He stared at her face for a long moment, then his gaze dropped to her hand. His shoulders lifted on a deep breath. "Deal," he said, clasping her fingers with his. He let go quickly. "But I'm still walking home."

FORD DIDN'T LOOK BACK when he heard the truck's engine rev up, or when the rattle of gravel announced a quick three-point turn and a rapid acceleration. He'd spent as much time as he could handle sharing the small space of the truck cab with Caroline. He wanted to clear his head before he had to deal with his sharp-eyed brothers. Teasing was a way of life with the Marshall boys—at the least sign of weakness, they would rib him without mercy.

He wasn't sure he could defend himself. Because, as pretty as she had been in high school—and he well remembered lying in the dark in the room he'd shared with Wyatt, thinking about the curve of her hips and the swell of her breasts and the cute round butt she got from being a damn fine barrel racer—Caroline Donnelly was a hell of a beautiful woman now.

The years had refined the elegant bone structure of her face, setting her eyes deeper, sculpting her lips into a delicious smile. Because she didn't ride as much, her legs were long and slim, shown to advantage by the short skirt of the dress she'd worn today. He'd had to get out of the truck and walk away before she saw how he felt about her. How he'd always felt.

Not that Caroline would consider dating him, even though he wasn't one of "those poor Marshall boys" now. Her boyfriends in high school had been the "cool" guys, the ones with nice cars, stylish clothes and plenty of money to spend on their girlfriends. He'd watched them all from a distance, overheard details about the parties, the skiing trips and concerts and vacations. He knew, because his dad talked about it, how fancy the Donnelly house was, how the barn had heated water dispensers in the stalls and, incredibly, a swimming tank for the horses.

His dad also described life for Caroline and her brother Reid—expensive ponies to ride and train on, handmade saddles and custom bridles and boots, clothes that never seemed to get worn twice. Their vehicles, in high school, were pricey pickup trucks with all the latest gadgets. Nothing was too good for the Donnelly kids.

Ford had made money over the years, but there was still a big gap between his family's status and hers. George Donnelly had earned his fortune by producing world-class quarter horses. He and his family socialized with the governors of Wyoming and Texas as well as princes of countries in the Middle East. The Circle M Ranch sold grass-fed, all-natural beef in a few Western states—not the same scale at all. And Ford's own luxuries—the Mercedes, good suits, a nice apartment—did not compare to the Donnelly empire.

Caroline attracted him, distracted him and reminded him of the part of his life where the Marshall brothers counted for next to nothing. A part he would prefer to forget.

So he would be happy if she stayed away from the Circle M. Her plan was too big, anyway, too demanding, too risky. He'd come home to take care of his brothers and do some relaxing of his own before getting back to the career he'd worked so hard to build. End of story.

Feeling better for having sorted out his problems, Ford reached the house and climbed the porch steps.

As the screen door fell shut behind him, his youngest brother walked into the living room with a sandwich in one hand and a soda in the other.

"So what's this I hear about teenagers staying at the ranch for the summer?" Dylan dropped down onto the couch. "Are we going to have extra hands this year?"

"Not if I can help it." Ford sat in the recliner near the fireplace and put up the footrest. "Caroline gave me the hard sell at lunch, but I told her this isn't a good time for us to be experimenting with a summer camp at the Circle M."

"I'd be hard put not to buy whatever that woman had to offer. She's a beauty, and a sweetheart, besides."

Ford unclenched his jaw. "You two would make a great couple."

Dylan grinned at him. "Thought that would get to you. You looked pretty starstruck when she walked over this morning."

"Eat your lunch. I'm taking a nap." He closed his eyes, hoping his little brother would get the message and drop the subject.

"Not that I want a bunch of kids hanging around," Dylan continued. "I've got a show coming up and the work's not half-finished. Playing babysitter doesn't fit into my plan for this summer at all." When Ford didn't answer, he went on. "But if Garrett is on Caroline's side, then it comes down to the boss's opinion, I guess. What do you think Wyatt will say?"

"About what?" Wyatt stood in the doorway to the back of the house.

Ford sat up again. "You don't have your brace on. You're not supposed to walk around like that."

"Yeah, well." He made a rude hand gesture, which dismissed the doctor's orders. "What's this I'm supposed to have an opinion about?"

Honey sidled around Wyatt and came over to the recliner to get her shoulders and ears scratched. Ford obliged and then got to his feet. "I'll explain after we get you tacked up, so to speak. I'll fetch the saddle."

Just as he'd finished strapping on the brace, Garrett showed up. "I'm starving—nobody offered to feed their preacher this afternoon. Did you leave the fixings out, Dylan?"

Wyatt snorted. "When does he ever put them away?"

"Just thinking somebody else might be hungry," Dylan said nonchalantly. "Saving them some trouble."

"Yeah, right." Wyatt took the recliner across from the

one Ford had claimed. "So are you going to tell me what's going on?"

"I'll let Garrett explain. I don't want to bias the jury."

"That's lawyer-talk for…?"

"Garrett supports the idea. He'll give you the official sales pitch."

Bearing a plate with a sandwich and a glass of milk, the man in question sat in the rocking chair, which was the only piece of furniture they'd brought from their childhood house.

"It was my idea, actually. Caroline was talking about trying to find something for the kids to do over the summer, to keep them out of trouble. And I suggested using the Circle M as a place for them to hang out, to learn and mature." Between bites and gulps, he outlined the proposal with almost as much enthusiasm and optimism as Caroline had shown.

Ford had to admit he'd enjoyed the explanation a lot more when he was listening to her, watching the shine in her eyes, the tilt of her head when she'd smiled—yet another reason he wanted the entire idea to go away. Next summer, when he wasn't around, they could work on this project. Wyatt could handle Caroline and her teenagers.

Maybe Wyatt would fall for Caroline. Or maybe Garrett already had, and that was why he was pushing the plan.

"Ford, I can tell by your face that you're not in favor of this program." Wyatt stroked Honey's head where it rested on his knee. "What are the arguments against the idea?" His mouth twisted with pain. "Wait a minute. I feel like I'm falling backward, trying to sit in this chair. Garrett, let me have the rocker." He struggled to stand up as the brace kept his spine straight and prevented any twisting or bending between his neck and his hips. "Thanks."

Honey looked at the new arrangement and opted to stay where she was with a different knee under her chin.

"Yeah, what are the arguments?" Garrett said. "I'm seeing only good things—the chance to help some kids to lead better lives and bring in extra hands for all the work around here. Where's the downside?"

Ford went through his objections yet again. "The legal liability is a big problem. If one of those kids gets hurt—the way you are, for instance, and you've been riding practically you're whole life—then I don't care what form the parents have signed, they're going to come at us with a costly lawsuit."

"Spoken like a true legal eagle." Garrett had moved into his usual defensive position, sitting forward in the chair with his elbows resting on his knees and his hands gripped together. "Not everybody is so sue-crazy."

Relaxed in the recliner, Ford kept his hands loose, his expression neutral. "Both you and Caroline have mentioned that these kids come from families with financial problems. Wave a hundred thousand dollars in their faces and see what kind of crazy they become."

"I say it's worth the risk."

"You're an optimist. I'm a realist, and it's my job to protect our investments."

"Since you're the one with the big salary. Got it."

"Since," Ford fired back, "I never again want to wonder whether we have to go to bed hungry because we don't have the money to buy food."

Wyatt flinched. Garrett looked down at his hands.

"Not a problem these days," the boss said in a quiet tone. "We're all adults. We can all work. Most of the time, anyway," he added.

A few moments of silence allowed the air to clear. "In my opinion, the setup is too ambitious," Ford said, finally, calmly. "A few hours a day for a week, maybe. But to have the kids living out here, making us responsible for them 24/7, is asking too much of us and them. When are we supposed to get actual ranch work done? What if a kid smuggles drugs onto the ranch? Or raids the liquor cabinet? If one of them runs away, we are responsible. With males and females in the group, it's even possible a girl might get pregnant. Do we want that culpability?"

All three of his brothers winced. "That seems unlikely," Garrett said. But he sounded less sure.

After a minute of silence, Wyatt pushed himself out of the rocking chair. "I'm going outside for a while to think. No, I don't need supervision," he said, as Ford looked at him in question. "I can manage on my own. I'm gonna walk to the corral, talk to the horses. They make more sense than you three, anyway."

Ford watched through the window to be sure his brother got down the porch steps. Then he turned back to Garrett. "If you're supporting this plan because…because you've got a thing for Caroline, I'm sorry. I don't mean to get in your way. But—"

"She's something special, that's for sure." Garrett got to his feet. "But I'm on board because it's a chance to do something good for kids who need a break. I'm just sorry you don't agree." He headed for his bedroom, the signs of his hurt feelings easy to read.

"Touchy, touchy." Dylan stretched his arms before flopping down full-length on the couch. "I'm gonna snooze till the boss shows up again. Maybe by then it'll be dinnertime, and somebody will have cooked something."

Ford eased back in the recliner to nap a little himself. "You ever think maybe *you* could do the cooking?"

"Nope."

"Just wondering."

He did manage to close his eyes for thirty minutes or so. Then, between feeding the horses and Honey and helping Garrett with the spaghetti dinner he'd decided on, supper was on the table before they all got together again. Even so, they had to drag Dylan off the sofa to wake him up.

Fortunately, he was never grumpy when pulled out of sleep. "Looks good," he commented, sitting down in the dining room. "How come we only eat like this when Ford comes home?"

"Because he does most of the cooking." Garrett passed the big bowl of pasta to Wyatt. "So what's the answer, Boss? Did you come to a conclusion about Caroline's project?"

In his deliberate way, the oldest Marshall served his plate before answering. "Let's say grace," he suggested, and they all bowed their heads while Garrett gave thanks.

As they took their first bites, Wyatt said, "Henry MacPherson took me on, a teenager with no ranch experience, and taught me what I needed to know. He paid the wages that, for better or worse, kept us alive those first couple of years."

The glance he sent Ford recalled his earlier comment about going to bed hungry. "In time, he paid all four of us to work on the Circle M. He brought us here to live with him, and he left us the land for our own. He pretty much saved our lives."

Looking around the table, Wyatt held each of their gazes with his own. "I say we owe it to Henry to pass the favor on."

"Yes!" Garrett pumped his fist in the air.

Ford glanced at Dylan, commiserating in silence.

In case anybody had a question, the boss made his decision clear. "We are going to do everything we can to give those teenagers a summer they won't forget."

Chapter Three

Caroline spent the afternoon and evening riding an emotional roller coaster. One minute she'd remember Ford's infuriating insistence on walking home, his obstinate refusal to consider the advantages of her plan. The next minute she'd be wondering about the Marshall family meeting and what the verdict would be. She expected Garrett to vote for her. Dylan liked her, so maybe he would, too. Ford, of course, was a no. At least he had his reasons, wrongheaded though they might be.

So the outcome depended on Wyatt's opinion, and she couldn't predict what he would think. He'd been two years ahead of her in school, but he'd dropped out when he was sixteen to take the job at the ranch, so she'd never gotten to know him well. Among the people of Bisons Creek, he held a reputation for honesty, fair dealing and reliability. Her dad, of course, dismissed the Marshalls as not good enough to do business with. But then, her dad judged his friends by the sizes of their bank accounts. Caroline chose to use a different standard, though her self-determination had cost her the family and home she loved.

When the phone rang at eight thirty, she was eating her way through a pint of chocolate-chip-mint ice cream. Garrett had called her in the past, so she recognized the number of the Circle M Ranch. "Garrett? Tell me fast. Is it yes? Or no?"

On the other end of the line, someone cleared his throat. "I hate to disappoint you, but this is Ford."

"Oh." *Damn*, she said silently. *I've probably bruised his ego.* "I'm sorry. I was just so anxious. I'm glad to know you got to the house."

"I had a pleasant stroll, as a matter of fact. And you have the chance you wanted for your teenagers. Wyatt voted in your favor."

Tears stung her eyes. She swallowed hard, hoping they couldn't be heard in her voice. "That's...that's wonderful. I'm so glad. And I'll make sure you don't regret it, Ford. I promise."

"I already do." Before she could react, he said, "Garrett wants to talk to you. Have a good night." When he came on, Garrett was as relieved and excited as she had been. Celebrating with him, though, Caroline didn't feel as thrilled as she should have.

Ford already regretted the agreement? The kids weren't even there yet; nothing had changed. Was it just sour grapes, or was there something more to his words? And how would she ever find out?

Lying in bed, the lights out and chocolate-chip-mint replaced in the freezer, she asked herself the really important question.

"Why do I even care what he thinks?"

Luckily, she fell asleep before she had to face the answer.

On Monday morning, she went to the office early and tackled the paperwork, trying to get ahead of the never-ending stream of forms to be filled out for each and every case she handled. Her coworker, Randi Ames, came in at eight, as usual, and they spent a few minutes over coffee celebrating the acceptance of her project.

"It will be so wonderful for the kids," Randi said. "And you'll get to spend three months out there with four gorgeous men. Surely you can fall in love with one of them before the summer is over!"

Caroline blinked away a sudden vision of Ford's solemn face. "I hope not. That would just complicate the situation. I'll have my hands full keeping the teenagers under control. I won't have time for romance."

"There's always time for romance." Randi had recently gotten engaged and was now matchmaking for every single woman she knew. "It'll hit you when you least expect it."

"Don't bet on it," Caroline murmured, as Randi unlocked the outside door to the office. She was too busy to take care of a husband. There was so much she wanted to accomplish in Bisons Creek, so many people who needed a helping hand.

In fact, her first appointment of the morning was with Susannah Bradley, whose son, Nathan, was one of the kids she'd selected for the summer program. Nathan tended to be a loner at school, made grades lower than his test scores predicted and had a history of cutting classes.

The real problem with this family, however, was Susannah's repeated visits to the medical clinic in Kaycee and the emergency room in Casper. She explained the incidents as "falls" or "stumbles," but doctors had reported that they suspected abuse. Susannah refused to confirm those assumptions, but Caroline had convinced her to check in every few weeks, as a means of keeping an eye on the situation.

One of those visits was scheduled for today. But ten o'clock, and then eleven, came and went. Susannah didn't appear.

"I'm going out for lunch," Caroline told Randi as noon rolled around. "I'll be back by one at the latest."

"Be careful," Randi said, because she knew perfectly well that eating wasn't the only item on Caroline's agenda.

"Will do."

The Bradley family lived on the outskirts of Bisons Creek in a trailer that had seen better decades. Toys lay scattered in the dirt that passed for a yard, and a beat-up sedan sat in the driveway. Caroline hoped that Mr. Bradley wasn't home as she knocked on the door.

"Susannah? Susannah, it's Caroline Donnelly. Can I come in?"

After her third knock, the panel swung in a few inches. Susannah peeked out, revealing half her face. "I—I'm sorry I couldn't come today. I'm not feeling well." Her voice was soft, with an East Coast crispness to her words. She wore dark black sunglasses inside the house.

"No problem. I was out of the office and thought I would stop by." A little girl appeared at hip level, and Caroline smiled at Nathan's five-year-old sister. "How are you today, Miss Amber?"

"Good." Amber played with the ears of the stuffed bunny she clutched to her chest. "But Mommy's head hurts."

"I'm sorry to hear that." Caroline looked back at Susannah. "Do you get migraines?"

"Yes. Sometimes." She adjusted the set of the lenses on her face. "The light bothers my eyes."

Caroline discounted the lie, putting a hand over Susannah's fingers as she clutched the edge of the door. "Are you okay? Do you want to see a doctor? I can drive you to Kaycee."

"Thank you, but it's not necessary. Amber is great, and Nathan is okay. Really, everything is…fine."

"Do you need somewhere else to live for a while? We have resources…"

Susannah shook her head. "I…can't. The kids…" She seemed to want to say more, but nothing came.

Dropping her hand, Caroline swallowed her disappointment. "I've got some news on that front, actually. Remember the summer ranch program I was hoping to start? I got the go-ahead yesterday, and I'm planning to have everything in place so we can start next week. Nathan will be spending twelve weeks on the Circle M Ranch, learning and enjoying himself."

"Oh, that's wonderful." Susannah lifted the edge of her shades to wipe her eye, and Caroline caught a glimpse of an ugly bruise. "He'll be so excited. He won't say so, of course. But I could tell when he talked to you about it that he wanted to be part of the program. As long as…as his dad says it's okay."

"I'd be glad to talk to him—"

"Oh, no. No, that wouldn't be— It'll be fine. I'm sure it will."

Caroline couldn't help trying once more. "You don't have to stay. I can take you to a safe place."

Susannah glanced down at Amber and stroked a hand over the girl's blond curls. "Things will be better. Travis has a chance at a job with your dad, as a matter of fact. If he gets it, we'll be doing well."

That was bad news, as far as Caroline was concerned. Her dad was notoriously hard on his employees, especially the ranch hands. But maybe the work would keep Susannah's husband out of the house more. "I wish I could put in a recommendation, but…"

"I know. Your dad is making a mistake, cutting you off. I hope he'll regret it, and the two of you can reconcile." She gave a small wave and withdrew into the shadows. The door shut with a rickety thud.

Driving back to town, Caroline consoled herself with the knowledge that she wouldn't be losing contact with

Susannah Bradley as long as her son was at the Circle M for the summer. And helping Nathan might add some energy to the situation; might inspire Susannah to improve her own security and that of her children. Maybe his father would make more of an effort to control his drinking. And his temper.

"I hope so, anyway," she told her mom, when they sat across from each other at a table in Kate's Café. "Or maybe he'll impress Daddy and keep his job. It's a possibility, I suppose." She took a sip of iced tea. "Where's Daddy off to today?"

"He and Reid flew to New Mexico to inspect some young bull stock. I jumped at the chance to have lunch with you while they're away." Linda Donnelly folded her hands together on the table and tilted her head. "I must say, you're looking very pretty. Something special going on? Besides this summer program you're so excited about, that is." Her own dark hair and green eyes were Caroline's fortunate inheritance. "I can't believe you convinced the Marshalls to cooperate."

"Garrett Marshall concocted the plan to begin with and proposed it to me."

Her mother smiled. "You've been talking with him quite a bit, haven't you? Just business, so to speak?"

At just that moment, Kate herself came over with their sandwich plates. "Don't let her fool you, Mrs. Donnelly. She was in here yesterday with Ford Marshall. She's gonna have all four of those boys wrapped around her little finger before the summer ends!"

At her mother's expectant expression, Caroline groaned. "It's nothing. And Ford Marshall doesn't even support the project. We're all working together for the kids, that's all."

"Ford, hmm?" Her mom finished off a French fry. "I remember you had a crush on him in high school."

"How could you have known that?"

"Sweetie, you talked about him constantly. What else was I supposed to think?" She smiled at Caroline's appalled expression. "But he went off to school, so I assumed you'd find someone else. Funny that you never have."

"I've had plenty of guys in my life, thank you."

"No one serious."

"I don't have time for serious."

"Of course not."

"So," Caroline said with desperation, "who is Reid dating these days?"

Kate came to pour more tea. "Not me," she answered.

They all laughed, and the break allowed Caroline to move the topic far away from the Marshall brothers.

As they walked toward the parking lot after lunch, Caroline put her arm around her mom's shoulders. "Sure do miss you," she said quietly.

Her mother returned the hug. "Me, too. I hate having to wait until your daddy goes away to talk to you. But…"

"I don't want him yelling at you." Caroline kissed her cheek. "Just know I think about you every day. And I wish things could be different. But I just couldn't live by his rules anymore."

"I understand. Maybe one day he'll realize his mistake." The doubt in Caroline's mind was reflected in her mother's face. "I keep praying, anyway. For now though, it was great to see you. Take care." They shared another long hug. "I love you, Caroline."

"Love you, too, Mom."

Back at the office, Caroline worked until after four to finish the last of her appointments and the associated paperwork. She contacted most of the families of the kids she'd picked to participate in the ranch program and arranged for them to visit later in the week to fill out the forms. The parents seemed generally pleased, the teenagers less sure. She had to believe they would enjoy their ranch experience, no matter what doubts Ford might retain.

Keeping her perspective optimistic, she grabbed her purse and a clipboard and headed for the door. "I'm going to the Circle M to check out the buildings where the kids will be staying," she told Randi. "Garrett says all they need is some soap and water to make them livable. I hope he's right."

"With four big strong guys to help out, I'm sure you'll get those rooms whipped into shape in no time."

"One of those big strong guys has a broken back, remember? And one of them opposed this plan from the get-go."

"Who was that?"

"Ford, the lawyer. He kept talking about lawsuits."

"That *is* his job." Randi propped her chin on her hands and got a dreamy look on her face. "I remember Ford. Blond hair, chiseled jaw and those navy blue eyes. Oh, yeah." Then she slapped her hand on her desk. "But you were voted Most Popular in our class. You can twist any man around your little finger, Caroline Donnelly. Just go out there and make him melt!"

Caroline blew out a sigh and left without bothering to protest. Had she really been such a...a tease? Why did people remember the flirting but forget the A average, the service-club presidency, even the barrel-racing wins, for heaven's sake?

No, she'd never had a serious romance, because most men just wanted a good time. And good times were nice, but a relationship needed more. She'd already lost one family, and she'd seen many others fall apart. She wasn't going to build her own unless she could be sure it would last.

For that she wanted a man with integrity, a man she could depend on and trust to make the right choices. A man who would make her his partner, put his family first and take care of them with everything he had. When she found that guy, she'd see about getting serious.

Inside the Circle M's gate, she stopped the truck, rolled down the windows and took some deep breaths of clean, cool air. Then she put on new lipstick, ran a comb through her hair and prepared to greet the Marshall brothers with all the confidence she possessed.

RIDING TOWARD HOME, Ford felt every minute of his day on horseback, thanks to the aches in his calves, his thighs and his butt. It had been way too long since he'd spent time in the saddle. And tomorrow the real pain would set in. By tomorrow night, he wouldn't want to move.

But he and Garrett and Dylan had moved about a hundred cow-calf pairs to nice fresh pasture near the mountains. He'd spent the hours outdoors, soaking up pure Wyoming sunshine. His favorite boots still fit, and his jeans were even a little loose. Whatever they cooked up for dinner tonight, he planned to eat a lot of it. All in all, a good day.

"Race you to the barn," Dylan called, as he surged past on his Appaloosa gelding, Leo.

Ford shook his head. "Crazy."

Garrett blew by, leaning over Chief's black neck. "Loser makes dinner!"

Without a second thought, Ford flicked the end of the reins at his palomino, Nugget, and set out after them. He hadn't been in a horse race in several years—he'd be lucky if he stayed on for the half mile to the barn, much less caught up.

At the end, the three of them came loping across the last field and up the road, their horses neck-and-neck. Dust clouds billowed around them while flecks of foam from the horses came back in their faces. They passed the finish line—the corner of the barn—and only then saw the truck parked in front of the house. The three cow ponies all came to a sliding stop right beside Caroline Donnelly's bright red pickup.

It used to be bright red, anyway. Now a thick layer of dust had faded the color to dirty maroon. Caroline stood on the porch with Wyatt, watching with wide eyes, her mouth forming a big O of surprise.

"Busted," Dylan muttered.

Ford threw him a warning glance. "You're doing dishes."

Garrett said, "Him and me both."

Wyatt's glare seared them even from a distance. "Is this any way to bring in a horse that's been working hard for you all day long? I'd expect you three to know something about taking care of your animals, but I guess I was wrong. You can just go out again and walk those ponies till they're cooled off—a good twenty minutes, I'd say, after that gallop. Once you've unsaddled, rubbed down and fed them, you can get over here and wash Caroline's truck off. She's staying for dinner, so when you've got the truck clean, you can come in and start cooking. I'd like to eat by seven."

With a curt nod, he turned his back on them, opened the screen door and ushered Caroline into the house.

They didn't make seven, but by seven thirty Ford had finished his chores and managed a quick shower, plus a change of clothes. He started to shave but stopped himself with razor in hand. It wasn't as if he was going on a date.

In the kitchen, he checked the chili he'd thrown together, mixed a salad and took a stack of dishes off the shelf. Then, pulling in a deep breath, he went in to set the dining room table.

As he expected, Caroline stood in the doorway to the living room a moment later. "Can I do something to help?"

"Sure." He'd meant just to glance over, but he got snagged by the sight of her in the last rays of sunlight, with copper glints sparking in her hair, her eyes shining, her skin glowing. She wore a red-and-blue-patterned dress that stopped well short of her knees. The long length of leg above her blue leather boots was a lovely thing to behold.

Ford struggled to get his brain back online. "We're... uh...having chili and salad."

"Sounds delicious." She came to the table and took the stack of bowls. "I didn't know you could cook."

"Ford did most of the cooking before he went off to college." Garrett walked in, carrying glasses and silverware. "He figured out menus all of us would eat without getting bored. After working at the feed store, he came home and made dinner every night. We've never eaten so well since."

She nodded, smiling. "That's impressive."

Ford's face heated up at the simple compliment. "Yeah, but I hate grocery shopping."

Caroline shook her head. "See, I don't mind that part. I just make a list and speed through. I'll even put it all away when I get home. But when I come in at night, the last thing I want to do is make a mess in the kitchen." She shrugged, and he noticed her pretty shoulders in the sleeveless dress. "I end up eating cereal and bananas more often than not."

"Not much of a dinner." He was setting plates around the table, going in the opposite direction as Caroline until suddenly they stood side by side. They both moved back, laughing, and Caroline stepped forward to slide by, but somehow there wasn't quite enough room in front of the table, and their bodies brushed together, her back to his front, as she moved across. Ford sucked in a breath, only to catch the scent she was wearing, flowers with a hint of musk. He couldn't remember when he'd last thought a woman smelled so good.

"I'm starving." Dylan came in from the living room. "When do we eat?"

"When you put on a clean shirt." Garrett nodded at the dust and dirt he'd worked in all day. "We have company tonight, remember?"

Caroline shrugged. "Don't bother on my account."

Dylan held up a hand. "No, he's right. I'll jog down to the studio. Won't take a minute."

Grateful for the distraction, Ford escaped to the kitchen. He'd strategically set Caroline's place between Wyatt and Garrett, so it was Garrett who pulled out her chair. By the time Dylan returned, dinner was served, and Ford was able to sit down at a safe distance from their guest.

Which was when he discovered that he was placed directly across from her and would see her every time he looked up from his plate. He watched as she smiled at Wyatt, at Garrett and Dylan, heard her parry his youngest brother's flirtatious comments and witnessed, again, her excitement as she and Garrett and Wyatt discussed the plans for the kids. Even when she was giving serious thought to a suggestion, light danced in her eyes, like a smile biding its time. Ford barely managed to finish half of his one bowl of chili.

But worse was yet to come. Once they all declared they'd eaten enough, Wyatt used the table to lever himself to his feet. "I've got some work to finish on the computer tonight. But Caroline wanted to check out the bunkhouse and the manager's cabin, see what needs to be done before the kids move in. Ford, can you walk her over, unlock the doors, give her a tour?"

What could he say? "I'll be glad to."

Though he was anything but.

CAROLINE SENSED FORD'S reluctance as they crossed the front porch. As she hesitated at the edge, he took the three

steps down and then turned to look at her when she didn't
follow.

"Something wrong?" He glanced toward her truck.
"They got the dust off pretty well, I think."

"As if that was even necessary." She was embarrassed
that Wyatt had required his brothers to clean her vehicle.
"It'll be dirty again before I get home to my apartment."

"Apartment?" He tilted his head, gazing at her in the
cool blue twilight. "You don't live out at the ranch these
days?"

"Um…no. I have a place in Bisons Creek, the top floor
of the old Curry house. Remember it?"

"Sure. I'm just surprised, that's all. I thought you'd be
living at home."

"No, Ford. I grew up and moved out."

His jaw tightened. "Sorry. I didn't mean to make you
mad."

"Like you are?"

He held his hands out from his sides. "I'm not mad."

"You're clearly not happy to be showing me around. I
was going to apologize, but that'll take more of your valuable time. So let's get this done, and I'll be out of here as
fast as I can."

She jolted down the steps and stalked past him, headed
for the building on the other side of the barn that Wyatt
had pointed out as the bunkhouse.

"Caroline, wait. Caroline!" Ford caught up with her,
grabbed her arm and pulled her around to face him. "Don't
run away. Again."

Breathing hard, she glared at him. "I am not running
away. I didn't run away yesterday. But you keep backing
off, and I'm trying to give you the distance you so obviously want." She hated that saying it hurt enough to sting
her eyes with tears. "Let. Me. Go." She jerked her arm,
trying to get free.

His fingers didn't loosen around her wrist. "I'm not letting go, so calm down. It's like fighting with a butterfly."

She stopped, appalled. "I am not a butterfly."

"No, you're a really beautiful woman who's driving me crazy."

Her jaw dropped open in shock. She closed it and swallowed hard. "What did you say?"

Finally, he released her and slid his hands into his pockets. "I said you're beautiful. And you're driving me crazy. Because I can't think of anything I'd enjoy more than getting to know you very, very well." His rich voice went even deeper on the last few words. Caroline understood exactly what he meant, and a shiver shimmied along her spine.

"But," he said, recovering his normal, even tone, "flirting with you would be a bad idea. Wouldn't even be possible, with seven teenagers and my three brothers running all over the place."

Caroline put her hands on her hips. "Are you so sure I want to—to flirt with you?"

His grin flashed in the growing darkness. "Not at all. I'd have to earn it, which would be part of the fun. You'd have to concede. Also fun."

More images that would keep her awake tonight. "You've thought this all out in two days?"

"Herding cattle doesn't take much brain power."

"So you're not mad. You're just avoiding me because you like me too much?"

"Exactly. The fact is, I'll be leaving for San Francisco before the summer ends. You've got family and responsibilities here. I don't want to risk starting something we can't easily let go."

"I've never had such a backhanded compliment." She blew out a sigh and then took three strides away from him. "There's your distance, Ford. Now, let me see this bunkhouse."

They crossed a grassy area to the timber-sided building. Inside looked just as she imagined it would—a long, paneled room with a kitchen and dining area at the end closest to the door, sofas and armchairs and a television stand grouped together on the far side, and a separate bedroom with bunks arranged along the walls.

"This is perfect," she said. "Exactly what we need." Everything wore a fine layer of dust, but it wouldn't require much work to be ready for the boys.

Trouble was, trying to come up with impersonal conversation wasn't easy, now that Ford had said he was attracted to her. Every impulse urged her to explore what could develop between them. Her gaze tended to linger as he walked around the room, feasting on the sight of his square shoulders under a plain blue chambray shirt, the shine in his dark gold hair, the shape of his long-fingered hands. If he'd been "cute" as a teenage boy, he was heart-stopping, dynamite gorgeous as a grown man.

"Caroline? Hello?"

She realized she wasn't paying the least attention to what he'd said. "I'm sorry. I was thinking about…um, sheets and pillows. What did you say?"

"I asked if one of us should sleep in here with the boys, keeping watch, so to speak. Are these kids apt to run away?"

"I don't believe so." The possibility hadn't occurred to her. "They're not here under duress. This is supposed to be a fun way to spend an otherwise boring summer. And it's a five-mile walk into town."

"There are five trucks they could take, if we include yours."

"None of them is old enough to have a driver's license."

"I was a thirteen-year-old once. I would have killed for a chance to drive."

"You must have been a reprobate."

"Absolutely."

She smiled at him, he grinned back and there was a moment of connection when she was tempted—oh, so tempted!—to want more.

Ford glanced away first and turned his back to walk toward the door. "It's getting late. We should check out the cabin so you can be on your way home."

Biting her lip, Caroline followed. She didn't try to talk to him, didn't point out the stars beginning to appear in the sky or the thin line of pink where the sun glowed behind the mountains. He'd just shown her the rules. She would try not to break them again.

The girls would be staying in the former manager's cabin, a cozy building with a separate living room and eat-in kitchen plus two bedrooms. It wasn't as dusty as the bunkhouse, but needed some freshening up.

"I might try to do some painting, if you wouldn't mind." She didn't look directly at Ford as she spoke. "The pink and green bedrooms are kind of dingy. And the bathroom could use a face-lift. The girls will care about stuff like that, where the boys won't."

"No problem." He was keeping his distance, leaning against the doorjamb while she explored the bedrooms. "We can help with that. With four of us, painting shouldn't take long."

"The Circle M must have been a big operation to have a manager's cabin and a bunkhouse that sleeps eight."

"When Henry was younger, he owned more land and ran more cattle, which required more cowboys." He retreated into the hallway as she came toward the door. "But his wife died when they were barely in their fifties. They didn't have kids, so the heart just kind of went out of him. He sold off half his acreage and most of his cattle and managed by himself till he got older. Then he hired Wyatt. The rest of us came along as a bonus."

"I imagine he liked having you all around the place." She led the way into the living room. "You were probably the children they wanted."

"Maybe. Or maybe he was too good a rancher to let the place go to ruin." He opened the door for her to exit, and she made sure to leave a wide space between them as she passed. The fact that she had to think about doing so was simply wrong.

But she kept walking as he locked the door, so he had to catch up with her again. "Anything else you need to see?"

"No, thank you." Caroline wanted to crawl into bed, pull the covers over her head and pretend she didn't know Ford Marshall, wouldn't recognize him if he kissed her on the lips.

Which he apparently wasn't ever going to do.

At the door of her truck, she pasted a smile on her face and turned around to find him standing a double arm's length away. As if he didn't dare get closer.

The smile died.

Opening the door on her own, she climbed into the driver's seat and settled in before looking over at Ford. "Thanks so much for the tour. If it's all right, I'll be coming around after work every day this week to get the dusting done, set up the kitchen, that kind of thing. Don't worry, though—you don't have to feed me."

His solemn gaze met hers. "You're welcome to join us for dinner anytime. There's always plenty of food. And your face definitely improves the scenery in the dining room."

She couldn't bring herself to respond. Instead, she shut the door and cranked the engine.

He stayed where he was, watching as she reversed and headed out. Caroline glanced in the rearview mirror several times and could see him still standing there until a rise in the land hid the house from her sight.

Chapter Four

As tired as he was on Tuesday evening, Ford didn't notice the red pickup truck sitting in front of the bunkhouse until he came out of the barn with his chores all done. He stood motionless for a minute, fighting his impulse to go over and check on how Caroline was coming along with her dusting.

"She's working late," Garrett commented as he walked by. "I know you think this is a bad idea, but she's totally committed to helping those kids to a better life."

"She's out to save the world. I get it." He blew out a frustrated breath. "I just wish she'd picked somebody else to assist her with that effort. There are other ranches available in the area—her dad's place, for one. Why wouldn't that have been her first choice for a summer camp?"

Garrett stared at him. "I guess you wouldn't have heard what happened, since you weren't here at the time. George Donnelly kicked Caroline out of his house."

"What?" The news punched him in the gut. "When? Why?"

"When she went to work with the Department of Family Services. He said he wouldn't have her wasting time with 'those kinds of people' and she'd have to quit her job. Caroline refused so he told her to go and stay gone."

"What would possess a man to reject his daughter like that?"

Garrett shrugged. "Donnelly's always been convinced that he stands above the rest of us. He had strict rules for Caroline and Reid about who they could and could not associate with when they were just little kids."

"I noticed we weren't on their invitation list."

"You've got that right. Donnelly stopped coming to church when they hired me. Which wasn't a great loss, to be honest, since he only showed up on Sunday and mostly slept through the sermon. But Caroline doesn't have access to the family ranch or the family money anymore. She's lucky if she and her mom can get together for lunch once a month, when her dad's away for the day."

"Why would she give up her family for a job?"

Garrett looked at him with a wry expression. "Interesting question. You'll have to ask Caroline for her reasons." He clapped Ford on the shoulder. "I'll find something to throw together for supper if you'll make sure the water troughs are full. Dylan's feeding the horses."

"Will do." But instead of moving, Ford continued to gaze at Caroline's truck.

She hadn't told him, hadn't explained why she was living in town. He'd made an assumption that she still had access to her privileged background, still depended on her family for support. And she hadn't corrected the impression.

So he really had insulted her, and she'd had every reason to be mad about it. An apology on his part was definitely in order. An immediate apology.

Ignoring the horse troughs, Ford headed for the bunkhouse. He knocked on the door—he didn't want to scare her—and then walked in. "Caroline? It's Ford."

Silence greeted him, but someone had clearly been working hard. All the surfaces in the kitchen and living room were shiny clean. The door to the bedroom stood open, and a vacuum cleaner leaned against one of the beds. Caroline, however, wasn't there.

Going back to the barn, Ford topped off the horses' water, straightened saddle blankets on their racks, made sure the tack room was neat. When he couldn't find anything else to do, he walked slowly to the house.

In the living room, Garrett and Dylan sat on the couch, wolfing down sandwiches, with Honey sitting in front of them, coveting each bite. "Go get some food," Dylan ordered. "Caroline set out the sandwich stuff on the table, ready to eat. Just what you were hoping for."

Not exactly. "Great." Heading for the dining room, he dug deep for a smile.

Caroline sat at one end of the table with a half-finished plate in front of her. "Hi, there. Since you all were so late, Wyatt and I pulled out something to eat so you wouldn't have to cook. Hope you don't mind taking the night off."

"Not in the least." Ford stopped behind the chair across from her and took hold with both hands. "I appreciate the effort. It's been a long day." Especially after a restless night, though he wouldn't confess that part.

She started to stand up. "I can make you a sandwich, if you want. What would you like?"

He waved her back to her chair. "I'll do it."

She hesitated for a second but then sat down. "Okay. Help yourself."

Taking his time, he put together a roast-beef sandwich he wasn't sure he could eat, threw some potato chips on the plate and, because it would have been rude otherwise, took the chair across the corner of the table from Caroline. "I stopped in at the bunkhouse. You got a lot done this afternoon."

"Looks nice, doesn't it? I should get the bedroom and

bathroom done tomorrow. Then we'll be ready for the boys."

"Ready for the boys to mess it all up, you mean?"

Her laugh reminded him of water tumbling over rocks in one of his favorite creek beds. "Probably. I suspect I'll have to supervise some clean-up sessions while they're here."

"Good luck with that."

"Or maybe I'll get you to do it. They'll probably take orders from you a lot more easily than some dumb female."

"You're definitely not a dumb female, but I get the point. A show of force never hurts when it comes to teenage boys."

"You would know. People still tell stories about how the four of you took care of yourselves without supervision. Wyatt must have had his hands full."

"We had our moments." He thought back over the years, remembering some of the less disciplined Marshall activities. "But we all worked pretty hard to keep things together. And once we got into rodeo, we tended to spend our energy practicing, so we didn't have a lot left over to cause trouble."

She nodded. "That's just one of the reasons I believe this program will help the kids. When you spend your day riding, roping, moving hay and all the other work that makes up ranch life, you're usually too tired at night to cause trouble."

"I hope you're right."

"But you doubt it?"

"I'm reserving judgment. You've made your case with Wyatt, now we'll see how the evidence plays out."

Her green gaze suddenly held mischief. "Want to bet on it?"

"What would we bet? Not money." If she was living on a social worker's salary, that wouldn't be fair.

"How about…loser takes the winner on a date?"

"A date?" He gazed at her, noted the flushed cheeks. "You and me?" A very bad idea, because he would enjoy it too much.

"Not a lifetime commitment, Ford. Just an evening's fun."

He expected to win, given the odds that something would go wrong. "Okay. It's a bet."

"Great." She stood up and gathered their plates together. "I'll put this stuff away before I leave."

"No, you won't." He tried to keep his gaze away from the cut-off denim jeans she was wearing. "We've got a cleanup crew out there in the living room. Just leave everything where it is, and they'll take care of it."

"I don't mind."

"*I* would mind. Let me walk you out to your truck so you can be on your way."

In the living room, Garrett and Dylan were both slouched down on the sofa, watching a TV baseball game. They came to their feet as Caroline entered.

Dylan reached her first. Taking her hand, he pulled her close and kissed her cheek. "You are a woman in a million. Thanks for getting supper ready."

She blushed and shook her head. "I hardly did anything."

Garrett came in for a quick hug. "Hungry as we were, it was great just to dive in. You're the best."

Standing by the door, Ford cleared his throat. "Ready, Caroline?"

"Of course. See you tomorrow," she told his brothers, and led the way onto the porch. Her steps were quick as she crossed toward the barn, as if she was in a hurry to leave.

But Ford wouldn't let her go without hearing him out first. "I'll switch off the lights in the bunkhouse," he said as she started to pass by her truck. "You should be getting home."

She hesitated and then turned around. "Thanks. I hadn't intended to stay so long in the house, but I hated to leave Wyatt by himself. And he had trouble bending to get things out of the refrigerator."

"Thanks for helping him." He opened the truck door. "Before you go, though, I want to apologize."

Her brows drew together. "Why?"

He wouldn't allow himself to avoid her puzzled gaze. "Garrett filled me in on what happened when you came to work for social services in Bisons Creek. About what your dad has done."

Her face changed in the second before she looked away from him. "He shouldn't have… You don't have to worry about that."

"First of all, I hate hearing that your dad is being such a bastard."

She shrugged one shoulder. "At least he's consistent. And it wasn't just about the job. He hated that I refused to do what he told me to do. He's not used to that."

"I don't have much experience with parents, but it seems to me that he didn't want you to grow up."

"Oh, I could grow up if I did it his way—as the wife of some rancher he approved of, giving him grandchildren to dote on." She took a deep breath. "I admit—I had it easy as a kid. All I had to do was follow my dad's rules, and I was given whatever I asked for. But in college I got far enough away from home to see the real world, where people aren't kept like china dolls on a shelf. I realized I didn't want to be a possession, or a trophy. When I told him so, he cut me off."

"That's rough."

Her head tilted from side to side. "Lots of people have

it worse. I should have paid more attention to the Marshall brothers back in school, and less to my own concerns."

Ford cleared his throat. "Well, I apologize for assuming your life hasn't changed in all these years. I drew conclusions without thinking too much about what the truth might be. A teenager can make those kinds of mistakes, but an adult should know better. I misjudged you, and I'm sorry, Caroline."

She rose onto her toes and put a hand on his shoulder. "Thanks." Her lips pressed against his cheek—a sweet, simple kiss.

Without thinking, Ford turned his head and brushed her mouth with his. Caroline gave a small gasp. Time seemed to stop.

Then, in the next instant, he moved in again for more. More contact, more pressure. More of Caroline.

The softness of her lips was a welcome like nothing he'd ever known—warm, giving and tender. Her cheek was smooth against his fingertips, her hand on his shoulder trembling slightly when he covered it with his own. He wanted to go slow, to savor each touch. He wanted to be greedy, drawing kiss after kiss from her until they both fell down dizzy with the pleasure. She sighed, and he wanted to drink in her breath, capture the instant inside himself. He wanted—

A horse whinnied, breaking his trance. Ford lifted his head and realized exactly what he was doing. Where and, most important, with whom.

"This," he whispered, resting his forehead lightly against hers, "was not the plan."

"No," she agreed.

"But I'm not going to apologize."

"Please don't."

Instead he stepped back. "Good night, Caroline. Drive safely."

She nodded and climbed into the truck. Those shorts gave him a gut-wrenching view of her legs when she sat down. He clenched his fists to keep them at his sides.

And he watched, for the second night in a row, as her taillights gradually disappeared into the night.

"Not too smart." Wyatt's voice came out of the darkness near the barn.

Ford stared up at the stars. "No."

"It's not your style to start something you can't finish."

"I didn't—don't—intend to start anything at all."

"Then you just made your road a lot rougher."

"You can say that again."

Now she knew what kissing Ford Marshall felt like.

Like Christmas Eve, with white lights sparkling on a snow-covered spruce tree, mirroring the stars glittering in the wide Wyoming sky. Like a Fourth of July parade, flags waving and the band playing "Stars and Stripes Forever" while military veterans marched in uniform, proud of serving their country.

Like a dark room lit with candles, two people lying skin to skin on cool, crisp sheets, driving each other crazy with hands and lips and tongues.

Oh, yes. He had made her feel all of those things, and more.

She savored the sensations as she drove along Main Street. Climbing the stairs of the old house she now called home, Caroline recaptured the press of his fingertips against her cheek, the warm weight of his hand over hers on his shoulder. Eyes closed, she leaned against the wall and relived each moment of every kiss.

Once inside her apartment, though, she shut the door on her personal fairy tale. Ford had insisted there couldn't be anything between them. He didn't want to take the risk, he'd said. Typical lawyer.

But she agreed. She wasn't going to the ranch to fool around with a cowboy. She would be there to make a difference in young lives. After her privileged upbringing, she owed the world a huge debt. Helping other people, especially kids, was her way of paying it back.

As for Ford, well, she'd initiated tonight's episode by kissing his cheek. That couldn't happen again. He'd said he was attracted to her, so who could blame him for testing the waters? She wouldn't blame herself, either. His apology had been so sweet, she'd only meant to let him know he was forgiven.

From this point on, though, they would behave themselves. Strictly friends, they would be, and casual friends, at that. Ford would return to his job in San Francisco. She would stay where she was needed, here in Bisons Creek. Nothing had happened to change their plans.

Nothing at all, Caroline told herself. *But it would be so awfully easy to fall in love!*

WHEN CAROLINE SHOWED UP at eight on Saturday morning with paint cans and brushes, the Marshall brothers were ready for her with ladders and drop cloths spread over the floors. Ford took the bigger bedroom, for which she'd chosen a sunny yellow. Garrett and Dylan worked in the other bedroom, and Caroline was painting the hall bathroom. Ford figured he could keep himself in line with his brothers nearby and a paint roller in his hand.

Caroline brought a radio into the house, tuned it to a country station and began singing along. She had a nice voice, clear and on pitch, and she knew the words to almost every song, sometimes even singing harmony with the lead. Dylan could hold his own in the vocal department, and they made quite a pair, singing back and forth along the hallway.

She popped into his room just as Ford finished rolling

the first wall. "That looks terrific! Much better than faded blue. Will we have to do two coats?"

He cleared his throat. "I think the yellow is covering pretty well." She was so damn cute in her cuffed shorts and white T-shirt, already liberally marked with the tan color she was using in the bathroom. She'd tied a lime-green bandanna over her hair, and that had tan streaks on it, too. "Did you get any paint on the walls?"

"I did, thank you very much." She stuck her tongue out at him, but her eyes laughed. "I'm an enthusiastic painter. Really into my work."

"So I see." He was tempted to stand there staring at her, enjoying her pleasure in just being alive. Most of the people he worked with in San Francisco would consider a weekend painting walls a complete waste of time. They'd hire someone to do it and spend the day at the beach, or visiting vineyards in Sonoma County.

But Caroline was perfectly happy wearing herself out for the kids she cared about. That kind of commitment and exuberance was contagious. If teenagers could change, her joyful spirit would make it happen.

"This room is a lot bigger than the others," she said, as he started rolling the next wall. "I'll take the brush and do the cutting in, so you won't have to spend the whole weekend in here."

"You don't have to—" His protest fell on deaf ears. In the next moment Caroline had bent over to paint the edge of the wall next to the baseboard. Her shorts got even shorter, revealing creamy thighs and tightly shaping that sweet little rear end. Ford stood motionless, dry-mouthed and breathless at the sight. The combination of spirit, intelligence and sheer physical appeal all bundled into the package of Caroline Donnelly seemed likely to destroy him.

"Sorry to interrupt," Wyatt said from the doorway.

Knowing he'd been caught staring at Caroline, Ford felt a flood of heat over his face and throat. "What's up?"

Wyatt extended a hand holding Ford's cell phone. "This thing's been going off every few minutes for the last hour. Somebody named Price wants to talk to you."

Aware of Caroline's questioning gaze, Ford set the roller down in the paint tray and wiped his hands with a rag. "Sorry. You should've just turned it off."

"I did. He started calling on the house phone."

"Terrific." The weight of the stress at the office dropped onto his shoulders. "Guess I'd better take this outside." Calling up the office number, he made his way through the cabin to sit on the porch steps.

When he reached him, Andrew Price, the senior partner, spent ten minutes reaming Ford out about being gone and another fifteen explaining what a pain in the butt his clients had been all week without Ford there to buffer the rest of the firm. Most of the rhetoric rolled on by, though words describing him as "irresponsible" and "unreliable" tended to get stuck inside his brain. He promised to spend some phone time with his clients at the beginning of the week and to shorten his vacation if at all possible. He asked a diplomatic question about an upcoming yacht race and was rewarded with a fairly civilized goodbye.

Letting the phone fall into the grass at the foot of the steps, he propped his elbows on his knees and put his face in his hands.

Return to the real world. With a vengeance.

"Sounded pretty brutal." Leaning his weight on the stair rail, Wyatt came down the steps beside him.

Ford rubbed a hand over his face. "Could've been worse."

"How's that?"

"Could've been you." They shared a grin, recalling a

few of Wyatt's more spectacular tirades when they were younger. "Not a big deal."

"You get this treatment a lot?"

"No." He stood up and stretched. "I usually manage to keep my stick out of the fire."

Wyatt looked him square in the eye. "You don't have to babysit us, you know. We'll be okay."

"I want to stay." His heart lifted as he said the words. And then sank when he thought about the inevitable departure for San Francisco. "I'll smooth some feathers, make some promises. They can survive without me for a few weeks."

But he'd just had a demonstration—as if he needed one—of why he couldn't linger in Wyoming playing cowboy. Despite what he'd said, there had been references to "replacements" and "applications." He was valuable to the firm just as long as he made them money. If he stopped producing, they would cut him loose.

And he couldn't afford to let that happen. The ranch and his brothers needed the support.

So he wouldn't allow himself to get tied down here. Not with the ranch work, much as he enjoyed it. Not with a bunch of teenagers trying to be ranch hands, though that would leave Garrett and Dylan in the lurch.

And especially not with Caroline Donnelly. She didn't deserve the only kind of attention he could offer—the "slam, bam, thank you, ma'am" variety he'd shared with women in the past. As if that were even possible in Bisons Creek, where everybody kept tabs on everybody else's life. A woman's reputation still mattered in this town.

No, Caroline deserved to be loved and cherished every day of her life. The man who offered her forever would be fortunate, indeed.

That man just wouldn't be, couldn't be, him.

By Sunday evening, the Circle M was as ready for an adolescent invasion as it would ever be. The manager's cottage was painted, its beds made, its kitchen spick-and-span. Over in the bunkhouse, a big bulletin board now hung on the wall, a place for Caroline to post the charts and lists she'd been producing all week at work.

"Kitchen duty," she told Dylan, who had helped her mount the board. "I don't want to have to remind them to go to the kitchen—I expect them to look at the chart and show up."

"You do realize these are teenagers? At that age, I was being reminded to do something every time I turned around."

"We're still reminding you to do your chores." Across the room, Garrett was installing blinds on the windows. "Some things never change."

"Obviously, we should have had some of Caroline's charts to work with."

Caroline nodded. "Obviously. Part of the point of this camp is to give them strategies for managing their lives. Schedules, charts, planning…a lot of them don't get this kind of structure at home."

Dylan chuckled. "A week with Ford will deliver the message. He's Mr. Organization, for sure."

"He'll set a great example," she said, forcing her tone to remain enthusiastic. Since the phone call from his boss yesterday, Ford had been harder to talk to. She hadn't been able to get a single smile out of him for the rest of the day. And today she'd barely seen him—he always seemed to be working somewhere else. "All four of you will make excellent role models."

"Which means you'd better behave, Dylan." Garrett adjusted the finished blind and gathered his tools. "You're nearest to their age, so the kids will be watching you pretty close."

"I'm ten years older, for God's sake." He noticed Garrett's frown and rolled his eyes. "Sorry. For Pete's sake. We're not exactly peers."

"I'm just saying they'll relate to you better than the over-thirty crowd."

"Thanks for the pressure. I'll try to restrain my hedonistic tendencies." He stalked to the door. "See you at supper, Caroline." The door slammed behind him.

She looked over at Garrett. "You're a little hard on him, aren't you?"

The minister lifted his shoulders with a deep breath. "Yeah. But he's unpredictable—that artistic side of him can cause trouble. I was just trying to avoid problems."

"I understand." Stepping back, she surveyed the completed bulletin board. "I guess I've got as much paper on this thing as it will hold. I hope they like the poster." She'd put up a colorful rodeo flier featuring a cowboy riding a bucking bronc, waving his hat with one hand while he held on with the other. "I want them to know right away they'll be having fun."

Garrett came over and put an arm around her shoulders. "It looks great. You've done a terrific job in a short time. The first Circle M summer camp will be a major success." He squeezed her up against his side. "Congratulations."

The outside door opened with its distinctive squeak. "Dinner's read—"

Caroline glanced over to see Ford standing on the threshold. As she watched, his face changed from relaxed to rigid.

"Sorry," he said. "I just came to say that the food is ready. When you are." He turned away before she could take a breath to speak.

"Great." Garrett dropped his hand to her shoulder blade. "I'm hungry. I'll bet Caroline is, too. Shall we go?"

"S-sure." But Ford hadn't waited. When Caroline

reached the doorway, his long strides had already taken him halfway to the house. Garrett closed the bunkhouse door behind them, and they trailed Ford in to dinner.

Which was torture. Dylan avoided talking with Garrett, and that was bad enough, but Ford didn't have a word to say to anyone. Caroline had hoped to go over the details for the kids' arrival at the ranch tomorrow, but only Garrett was cooperating. Suddenly, his expectation of success struck her as wishful thinking.

But she wouldn't allow this project to fail. Pushing aside her plate with her beef stew barely touched, she propped her crossed arms on the table.

"I have something to say." She spoke loudly, determined to get everyone's attention.

Three pairs of eyes focused on her face, but Caroline waited until even Ford lifted his gaze to meet hers.

"I know that the decision to host these kids was not unanimous." She met the eyes of each of the four men in turn. "But I understand that the Marshall brothers stick together and give their best when they take on a project. So that's what I'm expecting now."

Dylan stirred in his chair. Ford didn't move.

"Despite disagreements or personal issues, we have to put ourselves out to show these kids a good time and, more important, to draw from them the cooperation and responsibility that will benefit them as adults. We're committed, at this point. We must be able to count on each other till the end of the summer. Can we do that?"

Dylan, to his credit, answered right away. "We can."

"One hundred percent," Garrett said.

Wyatt nodded. "Of course."

She drew a breath and narrowed her gaze on Ford.

"Whatever it takes," he said, at last. "I'll be here." His neutral tone challenged her to demand more enthusiasm.

Caroline wouldn't give him the satisfaction. "Great.

I'll help with dinner cleanup and then we can all get a good night's sleep. The kids will arrive at nine tomorrow morning."

Chapter Five

A white passenger van rolled into the drive in front of the house at exactly nine o'clock on Monday morning. Ford watched from the barn door as Caroline hopped down on the driver's side, ready for a day on the job in jeans, a chambray shirt with the sleeves rolled to her elbows and a white hat. She definitely took the prize for cutest cowgirl he'd ever met.

Not that he should be noticing. After flipping over and punching his pillow about a hundred times last night, he had decided that seeing Garrett with his arm around Caroline had been a good thing. Now he knew the truth, so they could get on with their romance, and he would just smother this inconvenient attraction. He had enough to take care of without getting tangled up in even the simplest relationships.

Meanwhile, trouble in the form of seven surly teenagers began to emerge from the van. They all looked pretty much the same—baggy pants and T-shirts on the boys, tight jeans and form-fitting shirts on the three girls. Each kid had a backpack slung over a shoulder and a phone in one hand.

Ford sighed and tugged his hat a little lower. It was going to be a long, hard summer.

By the time he reached them, Garrett and Dylan had

joined the group. They were attempting to make conversation, but the single-syllable replies from the kids dammed the flow.

As he arrived, Caroline gave him a big smile. "Good morning!" Then she turned back to the teenagers. "Guys, this is Ford Marshall. He'll be working with us, too. He's taken a few weeks off from his job as a lawyer in San Francisco to be here while his brother Wyatt recovers."

Ford nodded, the boys shuffled their feet and the girls tugged at their hair and clothes. Greetings concluded.

To the kids, Caroline said, "We can't have four Mr. Marshalls at the dinner table. So I'm thinking you guys can use Mr. Wyatt, Mr. Ford, Mr. Garrett and Mr. Dylan. Sound okay?"

Dylan rolled his eyes, but beyond a couple of shrugs, the teenagers didn't respond.

Caroline persevered. "And now you can introduce yourselves. Justino, why don't you start?"

Standing at the end of the line, the tallest boy sighed. "You just did. My name's Justino." He used the Spanish pronunciation. "Justino Peña."

After a stretch of silence, Justino elbowed the guy next to him. "Come on, man. Don't be stupid."

"Marcos," the next one said in a loud, irritated voice. "Oxendine." Shaggy black hair hid his eyes, while his bulky build predicted a lack of endurance.

"Thomas Gray Cloud." The name came quickly from a shorter kid with the ruddy complexion that announced his Native American heritage. "Call me Thomas. Not Tommy."

"Will do," Garrett assured him.

Beside Thomas stood a boy so thin, Ford wondered if he got fed at home. Sharp cheekbones and a high forehead made him look more like a poet than a cowboy. "Nathan Bradley," he said in low tones. "Nate is fine."

Dylan cleared his throat. "Glad to meet you guys." He smiled at the girls. "Ladies?"

The three of them giggled, of course. "Lizzie Hanson," the blonde said, twirling a strand of hair.

The redhead had freckles and a friendly grin. "I'm Becky Rush," she drawled. "Pleased to meet y'all."

Big, dark eyes and shiny, straight, black hair spoke to the last girl's Spanish pedigree. "Lena Smith. Why won't my phone work?"

Garrett laughed. "Our signal isn't great out here. You might have to settle for email instead of texting. Or use the house phones."

"You didn't say we'd be cut off from the whole world," Lena complained to Caroline. "I'm not living without my phone all summer."

Caroline took the declaration in stride. "You'll be busy," she promised. "You won't have time to miss texting."

From the muttering, it was clear the kids didn't believe her. A revolt seemed imminent.

Ford stepped forward. "Let's get organized—bring in your bags, set up your bunks and then we'll have a chance before lunch to tour the barn. Phones work better up the hill."

"Right. Come get your stuff." Caroline headed to the rear of the van. "Each person carries their own."

"Seriously?" Lena propped her hands on her hips. "With all these guys around?"

Lizzie dropped her bag after twenty steps. "I can't carry this all the way up the hill." She looked over her shoulder, fluttering her mascara-coated lashes. "Can't somebody help me?"

Dylan smothered a laugh, while Ford bit down on a smile. Caroline flashed both of them a warning glance. "No, I told you to bring only what you'd be able to carry. Take it in stages—you'll get there."

Groaning, Lizzie picked up her duffel and staggered on. Becky followed, blowing her red bangs off her forehead. Lena brought up the rear. "This is stupid."

Ford figured that was a phrase he would be hearing a lot of in the next couple of months.

The guys trooped into the bunkhouse and through to the bedroom, where there was an immediate traffic jam at the door.

"The beds aren't made!"

"We're not maids," someone else said.

"I'll sleep on the bare mattress."

"No, you won't." Garrett stood behind them. "You guys can all learn to make your own bed, so when you're living large as a single guy you'll know what to do. Just choose a bunk, and we'll get it done."

Marcos turned in his tracks, brushed past Garrett and stomped toward the outer door. "I'm outta here. Not spending my summer cleaning house."

Ford blocked his way through the door. "Chicken?"

The boy glared at him. "'Scuse me?"

From the bedroom, somebody made clucking noises. Ford nodded. "Sounds to me like you're afraid you won't measure up."

"I'm not afraid of anything. I got better things to do than make beds."

"You can sleep on the couch, not worry about making a bed. Now what's your excuse?"

"I don't need no excuse. I don't have to be here."

"Caroline thinks you do."

Her name softened the kid up a bit. He stared at the floor.

Pressing his advantage, Ford said, "She made a big effort to work this out for you. Put me and my brothers to a lot of trouble."

A misstep—Marcos's head came up in defiance. "That's *your* problem."

"The lady believes you're worth it. I'm expecting you to prove her right."

The boy muttered a curse. "This is stupid." But he turned and went to the sofa, dumping his bag and backpack on the floor at one end. "I'm sleeping here."

Garrett walked by. "Fine. The other guys have picked their beds and gotten the crash course on setting up." He pointed to the clock on the wall. "We'll meet you all outside in ten minutes." With a hand motion, he sent Ford outside ahead of him.

"That was risky," he said when they'd shut the door behind them. "You pushed him pretty hard."

"I thought the point was for them to be responsible for themselves."

"Your management style is a little…um…stern."

"Oh, and Wyatt's wasn't? I remember making beds when I was eight years old." Ford shrugged. "But hey, if you want me to stay out of it, just say so. I can get more work done—"

"No." Caroline spoke from behind him. "Of course you're part of the effort here. What happened?"

Garrett explained, and she nodded. "Yes, Marcos will push as hard as he can at the boundaries. He's probably the riskiest kid we've got here—I've seen him talking to known gang members."

Ford hooked his thumbs in his pockets. "You've saddled us with a gang member? Gee, thanks."

"I don't think he's committed, but teetering on the edge. I want to bring him back from that edge. So if you can manage to respect him while holding the line, that's all I could ask."

He met Garrett's troubled gaze. "And you think…?"

"*Chicken* was dangerous. If you can limit the insults, we'll be okay."

"I'll do my best," Ford said, knowing that it wouldn't be enough. The situation, which had just seemed troublesome beforehand, now appeared downright combustible to him.

Caroline's optimism, though, remained undaunted. "It was a great idea to give them the agenda for the morning. Now they know what they have to look forward to and the time frame for what we'll be doing. Keeping them busy is the key."

"Did they bring clothes to ride in? Boots?" He shook his head. "Those baggy pants and sneakers aren't safe on horseback. Just because we have signed releases, there's still a risk—"

"I know, I know." She held up a hand. "I made sure they brought regular jeans and boots."

"And can we confiscate the cell phones?" He glanced toward the girls' cabin, where the three of them stood on the porch communing with their electronics. "Otherwise they won't hear most of what's said or see what's being done."

"Confiscate? No." She grinned. "But I'll get them to leave the phones inside."

As she headed to the cabin, Ford called, "Good luck with that."

Garrett frowned at him. "You are such a pessimist."

"Realist. Teens can't breathe without their phones."

But a few minutes later, when the kids approached the door to the barn, no phones were in evidence. "How'd she do that?" Ford asked Dylan as they stood watching.

"Probably bribes."

"Yeah." The group formed in front of him, and Ford straightened up. Showtime. "I'd like to officially welcome all of you to the Circle M Ranch. A man named MacPherson built this property and left it to the Marshall brothers to take care of. We're glad to have all of you helping us in that effort this summer. We hope you'll have fun as you learn some new skills and discover what ranching is about."

None of them seemed particularly impressed. "Man, I don't want to be a rancher," Justino said. "Cows smell."

"What do you want to do?" Dylan shot back.

"I'm gonna be impressive, man. A rap star, maybe."

The kids laughed. "Yeah, cool."

"That's the road, man."

"Get the big bucks!"

"Good plan," Ford said, cutting through the comments. "So you can be a rapper who lets other people manage his life and his money…"

"Oh, yeah."

He continued. "…who lets them steal what he makes and send his career into a tailspin."

Groans and moans, denial and protests came in his direction.

"Or…you can be smart and understand how business works, where your money is and who's spending it."

Marcos spread his arms wide and glanced around. "And we're gonna learn that here in the middle of nowhere?" Thomas and Justino agreed. Nate had yet to say a single word.

Ford shrugged. "Music or cattle, the principles are the same—manage expenses, expand your market, grow your bottom line." He grinned at them and raised his right hand chest high, with the first finger pointed down. His voice took on a singsong tone as he quoted, "It's all about the money, yeah, the wheels, the Benjamins, the bling, ya know it's all about the money, gotta get you some, get you some."

The kids hooted and shouted as they heard the rhythm and lyrics from a recent, popular rap song. Dylan and Garrett laughed as the teenagers—all except Nate—started singing together, stomping their feet and dancing, using a few of the less savory words that Ford had deliberately left out.

He couldn't help but grin at the way they were enjoying themselves. His gaze went to Caroline, watching from the other side of the impromptu dance party. Her eyes were round, her mouth open in surprise.

As he watched, though, she looked directly at him. She grinned back, and her eyes glowed with something that might be approval. Whatever it was, he enjoyed the feeling.

Way too much for his own peace of mind.

JUST LIKE THAT, he'd captured them. Using their language, borrowing from a culture they understood, Ford had declared himself their friend.

And he'd captured *her*—with his grin, with a sense of shared effort and accomplishment. Caroline wanted to kiss him for what he'd just done. But then she wanted to kiss him regardless of what he did or said.

And that was absolutely the last thing she should be thinking about. The kids were what mattered, and, right now, Ford had them wrapped around his thumb. When he went into the barn, they followed, ready to hear more of what he might say. She brought up the rear with Garrett and Dylan.

"Can you believe he did that?" she asked them.

"Oh, sure." Garrett pushed his hat back on his head. "Ford's an omnivore when it comes to music. You might hear country coming out of his speakers, or classical or blues and jazz. Or rap, evidently."

Dylan chuckled. "I can picture him in one of his pricey lawyer suits, dancing hip-hop. He probably could get a recording deal, if he wanted one. He was always talented at music, just never had time."

Still amazed, Caroline caught up with the teenagers where they stood near the tack, examining saddles and pads and bridles. On nearby shelves, each horse had a bucket with his or her name on it and grooming supplies inside—brushes, hoof picks and mane combs among them.

"You'll meet your horses after lunch," Ford told the kids. "And spend some time getting to know them. We keep a good supply of horse cookies around for making friends."

"Won't they bite?" Lizzie asked, her voice squeaky. "I heard horses bite."

"We'll show you the right way to offer treats," Dylan assured her. "And we've picked out some of the nicest horses in the county for you to ride."

Glancing around, Caroline noticed the group was a little smaller than it should be—Justino and Lena weren't gathered with the rest. As Ford invited his audience to investigate lariats, branding irons and other tools of the ranching trade, she stepped into the aisle between stalls and walked silently along, glancing into the horse boxes. All of them were empty but ready, with clean straw on the floor and a rack of fresh hay awaiting each lucky occupant.

A giggle and a smooching sound alerted her to what she would find at the end of the row. Leaning against a wall, Justino and Lena were locked chest to chest, hip to hip, kissing as if the world was about to collapse around them.

Which Caroline planned to make happen. "Ahem." She stepped into the stall. "You two get lost?"

They broke apart, both breathing hard, red in the face. Neither of them answered her question. At least all their clothing was still in place.

Arms crossed over her chest, she stared them down. "You didn't mention your relationship when we were planning this experience. I imagine you thought you'd get to spend more of the summer together this way?"

Their guilty expressions confirmed her guess. "I understand that you care about each other and want to be close." The memory of Ford's kisses flashed through her mind. Again. "But you know you're not here to make out, right?"

With hangdog nods, the two teens agreed.

"And it's not cool to be crawling all over each other with everybody else around. I'm asking you not to act like boyfriend and girlfriend when we're in a work situation—only when you have time off. In private. Understand?"

Justino blew out a deep breath. "Yes."

Lena wiped tears from underneath her lashes. "I guess so."

"Not good enough," Caroline told her. "If you can't follow the rules, I will have to send one of you home. Then you won't see each other for weeks."

The girl gasped. "Okay," she said, finally. But her resentment was evident.

"After you," Caroline said, ushering them through the stall door ahead of her. "Let's find the others."

They followed the sound of laughter to the feed room, where Dylan was explaining some details of horse keeping. "Thermometer," he said, holding up that item. "Goes in under the tail."

"Eww," Becky moaned. "Not me. I won't be messing with horses' butts."

Caroline saw one side of Ford's mouth quirk, as if he wanted to smile. He stood to the side, shoulder braced against the wall, with his hands in the pockets of his jeans and one booted ankle crossed over the other—the quintessential cowboy pose.

Setting her teeth, she dragged her brain back to the conversation.

"Why does it have a string attached?" Lizzie asked.

Dylan tried to appear serious. "Sometimes the thermometer gets...um...sucked in."

"Oh, gross." Thomas groaned. "Just gross."

The other kids made sounds of revulsion—all except Nathan. He hadn't said anything since introducing himself.

"You brand the cows. That's like being burned, isn't it?" Lena wrapped her arms around her tiny waist. "Doesn't it hurt?"

Dylan gave the question serious consideration. "For a while, maybe. But the cattle have thick hides. They scar up pretty quickly and forget all about it."

"You *think* they forget." Marcos stuck out his arm to show an ugly scar. "I got this when I was seven, running too close to the fire. I ain't forgot how bad it hurt. You don't have any idea what cows remember."

"You saying you're not any smarter than a cow?" Thomas asked.

Marcos's fists came up. "I'm saying you're a—"

Ford straightened. "That's enough." His quiet voice cut through the conflict. "Marcos is right—we don't know that branded cattle forget. But they graze, sleep and drink the same as unbranded animals, so we're assuming they're all right. Meanwhile, it's almost time for you all to get fed yourselves. Show up at the house in fifteen minutes, and lunch will be ready."

"Yes!" With whoops and shouts, the kids rushed out, leaving Caroline and three Marshalls behind in the quiet of the barn.

"You'd think we'd been torturing them," Dylan said. "They're a tough crowd."

"The afternoon will be better. I hope." Garrett wiped a hand over his face. "Food will definitely help. Excellent strategy, Ford."

"Caroline made the schedule." He nodded in her direction, but didn't meet her gaze with his own. "I'm just following instructions."

She heard doubt in his voice. "We're off to a great start," she insisted. "They'll be thrilled with the horses this afternoon. And they'll be cooking their first meal for dinner."

"We can sit around the fire afterward, roast marshmallows." Garrett nodded. "Then get them in bed because they'll be up early tomorrow for breakfast and their first riding lesson. It's all going to work out fine."

"I hope you're right." Ford headed for the feed room door. "If we're going to serve lunch, though, I'd better find out if Wyatt needs any help. I'll leave you three to herd the kids down to the house."

His boot heels hit the floor with a solid thump as he walked away. Caroline glanced at Garrett. "How can he be so good with them and yet so dubious of their potential?"

Garrett waited for her to go ahead of him out the door. "As a lawyer, I guess he's seen the best and the worst kinds of behaviors."

"And knows that both can exist in the same person," Dylan added, following them.

Caroline couldn't restrain her protest. "These are kids!"

"Kids with issues." He clicked his tongue. "Not angels."

They came to the barn door and looked out. With the exception of Nate, the teenagers had gathered on the porch of the ranch house, taking advantage of the shade. And they were all focused on the phones in their hands, even Lena and Justino.

"But where is Nathan?" Caroline glanced over the area, from the door of the bunkhouse to the girls' cabin. "Why wouldn't he be with the rest of the group?"

"I'll check the bunkhouse," Garrett said, and jogged in that direction.

Dylan headed back into the barn. "Maybe he got distracted by something in here."

Hands on hips, Caroline surveyed the landscape again, searching for Nathan's thin figure. He was wearing a brown T-shirt, she recalled, which didn't exactly stand out in a landscape filled with brown and green. Where would he have taken off to? And why?

The barn sat at the top of a gentle rise, with the bunkhouse and cabin below it on the slope and the house even farther downhill. Caroline walked in the opposite direction, toward the broad landscape of golden plains that made up the Circle M Ranch. In the near distance she could see a bridge running over a rocky creek bed shaded by cottonwood trees. On the other side of the bridge was a gate with fences on either side running as far as the eye could follow. In the days to come, the kids would be riding across those fields, enjoying the freedom and excitement of the range. She couldn't wait to share the pleasure with all of them.

Movement in the corner of her eye caught her attention. To her left were the horse corrals behind the barn, where a colorful herd milled around, nosing the dirt, sniffing the air and each other. Outside the fence, Nate stood so still he might as well have been a part of the enclosure rather than a living boy.

She went to join him. "Nice horses," she said, as a greeting.

Nate nodded without taking his eyes off the animals.

After a couple minutes of silence, she took a guess. "Do you like horses?"

He nodded again. Finally, he decided to speak. "They're so graceful."

"Have you ridden before?"

But Nate shook his head.

Caroline started to suggest they head toward the house

for lunch, but as she opened her mouth, one of the horses walked toward them—toward Nate, specifically. It was a mare with a tannish gray coat that seemed almost blue, a color called grulla. She stopped in front of the boy and stuck her nose over the top board of the fence, seeking him out.

Nate smiled and put his hand to the soft muzzle stroking the mare's nose. In the time she'd known him, Caroline had never seen such a peaceful, contented expression on his face. Blinking hard to keep her reaction hidden, she didn't dare say a word as horse and human communicated in ways that didn't require sound.

Then she heard her name called from beyond the barn. She stepped close enough to set a hand on Nate's shoulder. "Ready to eat?" she asked quietly.

Blowing out a breath, he let his hand drop and turned, walking toward the house with slumped shoulders. Still standing beside Caroline, the grulla mare whickered.

"Is that 'Come back' or 'See you soon?'" Caroline asked. But like Nate, the horse ambled off. "Thanks so much for the vote of confidence," she called after it.

"A friend of yours?"

At the sound of Ford's voice, Caroline jumped and spun around. "Oh… No, actually. I found Nate here, watching the herd." She could feel heat in her cheeks and was sure she must look flushed and flustered.

"Yes, but when he appeared without you, we wondered if you'd thought better of this enterprise and run away."

"Of course not. I was just coming." She marched quickly past him, without checking to see if he followed.

But he came up beside her. "Were Justino and Lena making out in a stall?"

"How did you guess?"

"They got off the van holding hands. And the way they stare at each other…it wasn't too hard to figure out."

"You're a lot better with teenagers than you advertise." Caroline sighed. "I didn't realize they were involved. I hope it's not going to be a problem. We talked about how they're supposed to behave."

"You're expecting kids this age to keep their feelings under control? It's hard enough for adults," he added, his voice low and taut.

Struck by his intensity, Caroline stumbled over nothing and would have lost her balance completely if Ford's strong arm hadn't circled her waist. "Sorry," she managed, flustered yet again. "I should watch where I put my feet."

"Are you okay?" He hadn't let go of her yet.

"Sure." She pulled in a deep breath. "Sure, I'm fine." The kids on the porch were starting to look their way. Hard though it was, she stepped out of his hold. "Thanks. Let's get this lunch underway. Who's hungry?" she called, striding briskly to the house. She answered her own question. "Me, for one. Let's sit down and get some food!"

Holding the screen door for the kids to file through, she glanced back toward Ford, who was coming up the porch steps. Waiting for him, sharing another encounter on the threshold, would be the worst possible choice. Her heart still pounded from being so close to him before.

So she spun on her heel, stepped into the house and allowed the screen to slap shut practically in his face.

I GET THE MESSAGE, Ford thought, opening the screen door. *Hands off*.

Served him right to have the door shut in his face, though, after putting his arm around her. He'd have to keep a better rein on himself, or Garrett would be out for blood. Next time, Ford decided, he'd just let Caroline fall.

Of course, he'd get hell from his brother for that, as

well. Obviously, this was a situation in which he just couldn't win.

Tell me something I don't know.

Chaos ruled in the dining room, with kids reaching across each other for sandwich ingredients, chips or bread, all talking loudly and sniping at each other. Only Nate sat quietly. Dylan, Garrett and Caroline were pouring drinks and fielding complaints. Wyatt stood in the doorway to the kitchen, looking grim.

Ford remained unnoticed for about a minute. Then he put his fingers between his lips and sent out a shrieking whistle.

All noise, all motion, came to a halt. Every eye in the place was on him.

"This is a house, not a rodeo arena," he told the teenagers. "Yelling at each other while you're inside is not allowed. Plant your butt in your chair and ask your neighbor to pass what you want along the table. *Please* and *thank you* are required. Be patient, and we'll make sure nobody starves to death." He glared at each one of them in turn. "Got it?"

Most of them nodded. Justino said, "Geez. It's the food police." Lena nudged him with her elbow, and he subsided. "Okay."

Ford ate his own sandwich standing up in the kitchen with Wyatt. "Quite a crew," the boss commented. "You have your hands full."

"I believe I might have mentioned that when we were debating this craziness. Seven teenagers all at once is about six too many."

"Yeah, but one kid on his own would get bored. This way, they keep each other company."

"Terrific. We'll have one pair fighting, one pair necking and the other three providing commentary. Two of them, anyway. Nate doesn't talk, as far as I can tell."

"I noticed the quiet one. Skinny, too. Maybe nobody cooks at his house."

"Maybe." He noticed his brother adjusting his stance for the third time. "How's your back?"

Wyatt lifted a shoulder in irritation. "I can manage to throw sandwiches together without falling apart."

"You ought to lie down this afternoon. I'll take your brace off before we go out to the horses."

His brother muttered under his breath but didn't swear loud enough to be heard. Ford just grinned at him.

Dylan came through the dining room door. "Thanks for laying ground rules. The rest of us were a little flummoxed, I guess. Good thing you're here, bro." He punched Ford's arm before returning to battle armed with a full bottle of soda. Over his shoulder, he said to Wyatt, "You should lie down. You look tired."

"If another person tells me to lie down," the boss said through gritted teeth, "there will be bloodshed."

Garrett leaned in from the dining room. "You about ready to set these guys up with horses? They're getting restless in here. Wyatt, you should probably—"

"That's enough." The boss slapped his hand down on the counter. "I will thank the three of you to keep your ideas about what I should or shouldn't do to yourselves. I didn't ask for your interference, and I don't appreciate it." He left the kitchen with slow steps not anywhere near his usual smooth stride. His bedroom door shut with a louder thud than might have been strictly necessary.

Garrett looked at Ford. "The rebirth of the grizzly. Do you think he's in pain?"

"I think he's tired of being treated like an invalid." Maybe Wyatt regretted turning the ranch over to a bunch of rowdy teenagers. Or, quite possibly, any one of the pressures he worked under on a daily basis could have flared into a crisis. Ford reminded himself to find a few minutes to talk to his older brother, discover if they had a problem.

He heard a chair crash in the dining room.

Make that a problem *besides* the obvious.

Chapter Six

Nate let the rest of the group get ahead of him going up the hill to the barn. He'd been waiting all morning to meet his horse, but he couldn't go running up there like some little kid overjoyed to see Santa Claus.

His sister, Amber, would do just that. At five, she could get excited about the smallest thing—a butterfly in the grass or a bird on a tree limb.

Thinking about her should have made him smile, but he was too worried to smile. Their dad was supposed to hear whether or not he had a job today. If he did, things would be okay for a while. If he didn't...

Nate shivered, even though the sunshine was warm. He didn't know if he could stay here and just wonder if things were all right at home. His mom had made him come, said she really wanted him to take this chance. She'd insisted, so he'd given in.

But he was beginning to wonder if it was a bad idea. Maybe he needed to be at home, in case things got rough.

Then he walked around the corner of the barn and there they were. The horses. Two bays, a chestnut and two buckskins, an Appaloosa and that pretty grulla he'd been talking to before lunch. Kind and patient, every one of them, with their big, dark eyes and soft muzzles, but full of flash and fire, ready to take whoever asked on a race with the wind.

At the corral, Mr. Ford had climbed up on the fence. He sat on the top rail like falling wasn't even an option.

"Take your time," he was saying. "Talk soft, move easy. Horses react quickly to something that scares them, such as yelling or sharp movements. You want to be careful and calm and then the horse will be, too."

Lizzie shook her head. "I can't do this. They're too big."

"Why'd you come if you're so scared?" Thomas rolled his eyes. "You knew there'd be horses."

"My parents made me, of course." She looked close to crying. "I didn't want to."

Miss Caroline stepped next to her. "I'll be right there," she said. "I'll help you get used to the horse. We won't go any faster than you're comfortable with."

Lizzie sniffed and shut up.

"There's four of us, so we'll take you into the corral in two groups." Mr. Ford hopped off the fence. "The gate is over here."

He stopped in front of the gate and turned to face them again. "Big, important, unforgettable rule right here. Leave a gate the way you found it. When it's closed, make sure—and I mean check two or three times—that you leave it closed. If the horses get loose, we spend hours getting them back. In the middle of the night, if necessary. None of us enjoys it." He raised his voice to near a yell. "So be sure you close the gate." When he grinned, everybody understood he was serious, but not mad. "Okay, the first four—let's go meet your ride."

Marcos, Thomas, Becky and Lizzie went into the corral, leaving Nate outside with Justino and Lena. He moved near the fence to watch the process, see who got which horse. He hoped that no one else was given the one he wanted. The grulla.

Justino and Lena stood beside him, but they were staring at each other and didn't bother Nate. They got in trouble at school for kissing in the locker hall. Now they were holding hands behind Lena's back. Did they think they fooled anybody?

In the corral, Lizzie stood staring at the chestnut, which shone like a polished penny in the afternoon sunshine. Miss Caroline was petting the horse and talking softly, probably trying to ease Lizzie into coming closer. The horse itself couldn't have been much quieter and still be breathing. Nearby, Thomas frowned as he held the rope to one of the buckskins—he'd made fun of Lizzie, but Nate got the feeling he wasn't too comfortable with the idea of riding himself. Marcos looked more relaxed, stroking the neck of a dark bay. It was funny that Becky, with her freckles, got the Appaloosa, which had plenty of brown spots across the white of its hips.

The grulla was standing by herself on the far side of the pen, rear leg cocked and head relaxed, as if she was taking a nap. So far, so good. If they gave her to Lena or Justino, maybe he could convince Mr. Ford or Miss Caroline to let him trade.

Yeah, right. Like he could make anybody listen. Talking wasn't worth the effort, not with grown-ups. And once you started, you might say the wrong thing. It was safer just to keep quiet.

Mr. Ford left Marcos and came to the gate. "Okay, you three, come on in."

Justino and Lena jumped and separated, looking guilty. Justino stepped up to open the gate, and Nate followed Lena through. Justino hurried to catch up with his girlfriend, leaving the gate wide open.

"Hold it," Mr. Ford ordered. "What did you forget?"

Justino and Lena stopped, but obviously didn't have a clue.

"The gate," Nate said. "You're supposed to close it."

"Right. Everybody has to be responsible for checking. If somebody you're with forgets, take care of it, or everybody has a problem. Got it?"

Nate went back, pushed the metal gate to the post and made sure it latched, testing it, just in case.

"Great," Mr. Ford said. "Now let's meet your horses. Justino, yours is the dark buckskin over with Garrett." He pointed to the far side of the circular corral.

Nate held his breath. The next horse would be Lena's. Would she get the bay or the grulla?

"Lena, your horse is up next to the barn—we call her Calico, even though she's dark brown. And Nate, yours is—"

"Blue Lady," Nate said, starting toward the grulla.

Mr. Ford came up behind him. "How did you know her name?"

Nate shrugged a shoulder. "She looks blue. Just guessed."

"We usually call her simply Blue. She's a friendly horse."

But Nate hardly heard the words. He walked to Blue's head and held out his palm for her to sniff. The hairs on her chin tickled his skin, and he couldn't help but smile. Stroking the other hand along her neck, he felt the warmth of her body through the sleek hair. He loved everything about her—the black stripe down her spine, her dark legs and the one back foot that was white. Beside him, Mr. Ford clipped a lead rope to Blue's halter. "Lead her to a place on the fence, and I'll show you how to tie her up. Then we'll get her bucket, and you can do a little grooming."

Nate took the rope, though it seemed as if he didn't need it, that Blue would follow him because that was what he wanted her to do. The other animals were standing along the perimeter of the corral, all of them patient and quiet while a bunch of dumb kids figured out which end would bite and which end kicked.

"You strike me as someone familiar with horses," Mr. Ford said, showing Nate where Blue's bucket hung in the barn. "Did you grow up with them?"

Nate shook his head. "I read."

"About horses? In that case, you probably know more than I do." Mr. Ford reached into a bin and brought out some nuggets that smelled like applesauce. "Treats always smooth the process."

Nate put a horse cookie on the flat of his hand and held it out to Blue, who gently lipped it into her mouth.

Mr. Ford gave Blue a pat. "I'll let you enjoy yourself. Just yell if you have a question."

Taking a stiff brush out of the bucket, Nate began to brush in short, quick strokes that brought the dirt up out of her hair to be flicked away. Lady Blue got shinier and sleeker the longer he worked. And she stood quietly, flicking her tail at a fly now and then, eyes half-closed as if she enjoyed being groomed. Nate could have spent the rest of the day just brushing *his* horse.

Around the corral, though, things weren't going so well. Thomas's horse kept stepping away from him, probably because he brushed too hard and was in too big of a rush to get done. Mr. Dylan kept trying to calm him down, asking him to be gentler. But Thomas got more frustrated every time the horse moved until finally he threw the brush into the dirt and stomped toward the barn. Throwing the brush upset the horse even more, and Mr. Dylan had to spend time quieting the animal. Then he followed Thomas into the darkness inside the barn.

Marcos's bay horse was standing still, but it had its head up in the air, and its ears were twitching. Its black tail whipped from side to side—not lazily, like Blue's, but the way some people snapped their fingers in irritation. Marcos didn't seem to be doing anything wrong as he brushed the dark brown horse, but Nate had read that a horse would sense your mood and respond in kind. Marcos's impatience with the whole process showed in the way his horse acted.

Beside Nate and Blue, Becky and her Appaloosa seemed to be getting along pretty well. Becky talked to the horse as if it was a human being, which the horse seemed to appreciate. She was even combing the brown-and-white horse's tail, which Nate wasn't sure he would be brave enough to try at this point.

Closest to the barn, Lizzie still acted terrified. Even though Miss Caroline held the chestnut's rope instead of having it tied to the fence, Lizzie barely stood close enough to touch the horse with the brush. The beautiful animal was pretty much ignoring her, anyway, because Miss Caroline was keeping its attention. Lizzie wouldn't go near the rear legs, and she flinched every time the horse moved its head, as if it would reach around and bite her.

Meanwhile, Justino looked bored. He brushed the horse but didn't put much effort into it, so the dirt fell onto the hair again. Lena was a little more energetic and actually seemed to enjoy making her horse shiny.

Thomas slouched out of the barn. His attitude seemed worse, if possible, but he did pick up the brush and return to the horse, which sidled away. So he just stood there with his hands on his hips, shaking his head.

"The horse senses your emotions," Mr. Dylan said, loud enough for everybody to hear. "And responds honestly. If you're angry or frustrated, the horse gets worried, even scared. That's not going to help bridge the gap between you."

"Why should I care?" Thomas dropped the brush into the bucket. "In case you didn't notice, we use cars to get around these days. I can already drive. I don't need to ride a stupid horse."

Mr. Dylan stared at him. "So why are you here?"

"Hell if I know. My parents made me, 'cause *she* talked them into it." He jerked his head in Miss Caroline's direction. "Said it would be fun. I don't see nothing fun about standing in the dirt trying to brush some stupid horse."

Nate heard Justino mutter, "Got that right."

Miss Caroline tied the rope of Lizzie's horse to the fence and headed in Thomas's direction. But Lizzie screeched, "Don't leave me!" and made a grab for Miss Caroline's arm.

The chestnut horse startled at the noise and jerked against its rope, panicked because it couldn't get free.

Next thing Nate knew, all the horses were upset, dancing around on the ends of their ropes, trying to see what was going on all around them, whinnying and tossing their heads. Even Blue Lady seemed worried, and wouldn't stand still. The rest of the kids ran to the center of the corral and stood butt-to-butt, staring at the chaos around them. Except for Lizzie, who covered her face with her hands and cried.

Mr. Ford, Mr. Dylan, Mr. Garrett and Miss Caroline went from one horse to the other, making soothing sounds and petting them, until the animals calmed down. Nate quieted Blue himself, stroking her neck and shoulder until she relaxed. He figured that would be the end of the horse session for the day. Not a terrific way to finish up.

Instead, though, Mr. Ford came to the center of the corral. "Walk slowly to your horses," he said. "Yes, you, Thomas. Lizzie, you should go back to your horse, too. When you get there, just put your hand on the horse's shoulder. Gently. Stroke the shoulder, the neck. Talk in a low, soft voice. Doesn't matter what you say, just that you say it quietly and calmly."

Miss Caroline spoke up. "This horse, the one you're touching now, will be your friend for the next couple of months. You can say things to the horse you wouldn't tell anyone else. And the horse will never betray your secret."

Thomas rolled his eyes, petting his horse like he would an annoying dog. The horse gave a big sigh, as if it wished he would just leave. Lizzie put her fingertips on the chestnut, but the horse probably couldn't even feel her touch. Nate heard some of the other kids talking to their horses, but he couldn't understand the words. He hadn't spoken to Blue—he wasn't sure what he would say. So he just kept stroking her neck on both sides, and her shoulders and along her back, enjoying the shape of her, the way her ribs floated underneath her skin, the roundness of her hips and the firmness of her chest muscles.

"You're sweet," Nate said softly. "I'm glad you're mine."

Mr. Dylan came up beside him. "You've done great," he said. "You and Blue are meant to be together. We'll work with the horses again tomorrow, but for now you can head on out the gate."

The others were leaving their horses, too. Thomas was the last—he didn't seem as angry as he had before, maybe even a little sorry to walk away. Lizzie, on the other hand, practically ran across to the exit. Standing outside the corral, with the gate securely closed, the kids watched as the grown-ups untied the horses and took off their halters.

And that was when Lizzie should have been scared, because the horses took advantage of their freedom to act up—running around, hopping and bucking, kicking their hind feet into the air. At the far end of the pen, near where Nate had been standing with Blue, Mr. Ford opened another gate. He gave a short whistle, and the horses started trotting toward the opening. Not quite a stampede, but Nate wouldn't have wanted to get in the way. They flowed through the gate and, in the next minute, were galloping across a huge field, so big you almost couldn't see the fence on the other side, with all the grass they could want to eat under their feet. In a couple of minutes, each horse had found its place to graze, some in groups of two or three, some by themselves.

"So much for day one," Marcos said. "How much more fun can we stand?"

"IT WOULD BE helpful if they at least wanted to be here." Ford took a long draw on his canned drink. "How are we going to accomplish anything with the attitudes they displayed this afternoon?" He frowned at Caroline. "We were supposed to be able to get work done with these kids here. When is that going to happen?"

She didn't want to confess her own disappointment. "Today was rough, I admit. But tomorrow will be better. They're out of their comfort zone, so they're figuring out how to fit in." After giving the kids a free hour before starting dinner preparation, she had gathered with the Marshalls in the barn to review the afternoon's progress.

Or, as Ford described it, the lack thereof.

"Thomas settled down toward the end," Garrett said. "And Marcos will come around. Lizzie might be a real problem, though. She's clearly terrified."

Dylan wiped a hand over his face. "That chestnut is the smallest horse we've got."

Ford tossed his can into the trash barrel. "Can we borrow a pony from somebody? She won't be able to herd cattle on something that small, but maybe she could start with a pony and gradually work up to the horse."

"I'll make some calls." Garrett headed toward the house.

"I'll bring the truck up for the hayride." Dylan put his hat on. "Will the boys want to help move hay bales?"

"Nate is on the dinner crew," Caroline reminded him. "But the other three certainly could be put to good use.

Give Becky a chance, too. Girls can move bales, you know." She sent him a smile.

"But they shouldn't have to." Dylan winked at her and left the barn.

Then she was alone with Ford, who stood staring at the floor with his face set in stern lines. She couldn't help asking, "What are you thinking?"

His eyes met hers. "I'm wondering if you have an exit strategy for this situation."

"You believe it's that bad?"

"Most kids enjoy horses. What happens if they don't adjust? How is any of the rest of this project going to come together if we can't put them in the saddle and take them around the ranch?"

"We have to be patient, Ford. Give them time. That's the whole point."

"I don't have time." The words seemed to emerge against his will. He held up his hand in apology. "Sorry. That's not your problem. But I'm not sure your patience is going to be enough."

Taking a risk, she stepped close and put a hand on his upper arm. "Two weeks, Ford. Let's give them two weeks to experience the positive side of being here. If they haven't made real progress, if they're not working together as a group, I'll swallow the embarrassment of failure and take them home. Deal?"

Being so near, she could smell his aftershave, see the fineness of the skin across his cheekbones and the flecks of gray in those deep blue eyes. Every breath brought in his scent, and she was dizzy from trying not to inhale deeply.

He lifted her hand in his free one. "So that's the bet now? Two weeks?" His fingers around hers were warm and dry, strong yet gentle. She could imagine them roaming her body...

A blush heated her face and throat. Caroline backed up abruptly, pulling her hand free. "That's it. But don't go assuming you're going to win. I'm betting tomorrow will show us some improvement." She sounded panicked, which was how she felt. "I'll catch up with you at dinner, okay?"

Without waiting for his answer, she spun around and hurried through the barn door. Clearly, when it came to Ford, she couldn't let herself off the leash, not even the least little bit. He went to her head like whiskey. She couldn't afford to get any more intoxicated.

He'd already ruled out a summer fling between them, even if it were possible, which it wasn't. And what hope could she hold on to for a lasting relationship? His life revolved around the high salary and exalted status of a San Francisco law firm. He thrived on conflict and control, which was not all that different from her dad's way of life.

A way of life she had deliberately rejected. If being with Ford meant returning to that world, she would have to refuse, or betray her most basic values. So…

He'd be leaving. She'd be staying. That was all there was to say about the situation.

Too bad her heart was not in the mood to listen.

SHAKING HIS HEAD, Ford watched Caroline scurry out of the barn. Just touching her fingers was enough to make his pulse race. He wasn't sure he'd be able to keep his sanity over the coming weeks, being with her all day, every day. Even knowing that Garrett cared about her didn't seem to matter. Ford might fight his brother for the right to hold Caroline's hand. How much more despicable could he get?

At least it would only be for two weeks. He really didn't believe these kids could make it any further. He admired Caroline's optimism and her commitment to rescuing kids on the verge of trouble. Her idealism appealed to the part of him that cared about justice, equality before the law and a fair chance for everyone to succeed.

But there was only so much that could be done. The kids had arrived at the ranch bearing huge burdens of resentment, self-doubt and anxiety. Horses and physical challenges could work wonders, but some of these teenagers needed more than the Marshalls and the Circle M could offer. Ford only hoped Caroline wouldn't be too hard on herself when the program didn't live up to her expectations.

Meanwhile, he'd be satisfied if everybody came through without injuries or stolen property. He wouldn't expect more.

Hearing the hay truck rumbling in the distance, he left the barn for the house to round up the hay movers. He found Caroline supervising Lena, Lizzie and Nate in the kitchen, while the other four lounged around the television, staring at their phones.

"I'm in search of a few good men," he announced. Then he remembered what Caroline had said to Dylan. "Or women, if they're available."

No one glanced up. "For what?" Justino asked.

"Moving hay. The cowboy way of strength training."

Lying prone on the couch, Marcos groaned. "I don't think so."

But Becky clicked off her phone and stood. "I'll do it."

Ford surveyed the three boys. "You guys are going to let a girl beat you?"

Thomas shrugged. "Who cares?"

Reminding himself that he was the adult in the room, Ford held his temper. "The rule on this ranch is, if you don't work, you don't eat." He heard Caroline gasp behind him. She believed he'd made a threat he couldn't enforce.

But she would be wrong about that. "So who wants to skip dinner?"

Marcos challenged him with a measuring stare. "You can't starve us."

"From the looks of you, it would take you a while to starve. I suspect by the next meal you'll be hungry enough to cooperate." Now he had Thomas's attention, and Justino's, too. "I'm not unreasonable—come work up a little sweat, and you're guaranteed a place at the table." He glanced over at the kitchen, sending Caroline a reassuring nod. "What have you got to lose?"

They held out for another couple of minutes. Ford leaned against the wall, crossed his arms and waited.

Finally, Becky broke into the silence. "Oh, come on. Don't be such losers."

The three boys stirred and slowly got to their feet. "All right, all right." Thomas headed for the door. "Let's get this over with so he'll leave us alone."

Ford followed Marcos, the last of them, to the door. Just before he left he glanced at Caroline, who was watching with an expression part impressed, part exasperated.

He winked at her and shut the door behind him.

Dinner was rowdy and loud, though for the most part the kids remembered his lecture at lunch on staying in their seats and using their manners. The members of the hay crew were full of tales about their exploits—how many bales they'd lifted, how much each bale weighed, who could lift the highest and throw the farthest. Becky had sustained her end of the work, and was pleased to recount for Lena and Lizzie how she'd kept up with the boys. Marcos and Thomas had competed, of course, but came out even, which was just as well for the general morale.

"Would you really have made them miss dinner?" Caroline came to stand beside him as he ate spaghetti and meat sauce leaning against the kitchen counter.

She was gazing up at him, but he kept his eyes on the kids at the table. "What do you think?"

"I guess that's your version of tough love."

"I'm not quite ready to use the word *love* with any of these kids just yet. But I had to get their attention. Teenage boys do have to eat. I remember being hungry all the time at that age."

"Meanwhile, teenage girls are trying to starve themselves to attract the boys' attention. There's something wrong with that picture."

"Maybe just the fact that they get involved with each other so young these days." He glanced at Justino and Lena, who were obviously holding hands under the table. "We push sex at them way too soon."

"So true. How are we going to keep those two apart?" Caroline was watching the young couple, as well. "I have no doubt they're making plans to meet in the barn after curfew."

"We'll have to watch them till they're asleep."

"These are teenagers. They can stay up all night."

"Here's a thought—they could do as they're told." Caroline laughed, and he joined her. "No, you're right. I don't believe it, either."

But now he'd looked at her, shared her good humor, and with that connection came an avalanche of the very emotions he didn't want to experience—the wanting and needing, the aching for more than just the occasional conversation. Her eyes widened, and the sweet blush in her cheeks revealed she felt the same.

Ford cleared his throat and pulled his gaze away. "So who is riding herd on the cleanup crew? It's going to be a tough job."

"I'll do it." Caroline put her own plate on the counter by the sink. "You've been the bad guy already today. Let me try to coax them into cooperating."

"Don't be afraid to call for reinforcements." He set his

plate down on hers and crossed to the door. Under his breath, he added, "You're going to need them."

MARCOS CAUSED THE first disruption. "I ain't washing dishes." With that flat announcement, he walked to the sofa, threw himself down and closed his eyes.

Thomas followed him. "That's woman's work." He dropped into an armchair and took out his phone.

"I'm not cleaning up all by myself," Becky said loudly. "This is a big mess."

"Get Lena and Lizzie," Justino suggested. "They can help."

Caroline stalked over to switch off the television. "Did you eat supper, Thomas? Marcos? Justino?"

None of them answered.

"Lena, Lizzie and Nate cleaned up the kitchen after they cooked your food. Now it's your responsibility to get it ready for breakfast tomorrow morning."

Thomas shook his head. "Ain't happening."

"Do you remember Judge Henley? Do you recall the plans she had for your summer?"

Justino stirred in his chair. Marcos opened his eyes to eye her warily.

"Right. After the three of you got caught stealing from the gas station, the judge recommended community service five days a week, eight hours a day. Do you understand why you're not out there cleaning up litter on the side of the road?"

The three boys glanced at each other.

"Because," Caroline said, "I told her you would be here, acting like model citizens while learning ranch skills. I promised you would cooperate and follow the rules."

Walking to the bulletin board, she pointed to the chart that indicated cleanup duties for tonight's dinner. "These are the rules, which say that the four of you are washing up. Now, you can wash dishes. Or you can pick up litter every weekday, all summer long. Your choice."

Justino got up first. "This is stupid." He started for the kitchen. "Come on, Marcos. You're no better than me."

"Man, my mom cleans houses, does other people's dishes. I don't have to."

Caroline gazed at him. "You're saying your mother has to but you don't?"

"No. I mean—" He scrubbed his face with his hands. "She don't make me do this at home."

"Lucky you. Eventually, though, you're going to have to clean up a kitchen. Might as well be now. Thomas, you, too." If they still refused, she didn't know how to compel them. And if she couldn't get them to do the chores, there really wasn't a point to the entire project. As Ford suggested, she might as well give up and take the kids home. Heaving a deep breath, Thomas stood up. "Let's do this, Marcos. I can't go back home and spend all summer hiding the old man's whiskey. Washing dishes isn't the worst job in the world. We could have to be taking all those horses' temperatures."

Marcos went into the kitchen. "Yeah, sticking thermometers up horses' butts. What a lousy job that would be."

The humor went quickly downhill, but as long as they were getting soap on dishes and rinsing it off, Caroline could stand it.

"At least they were talking about the horses," she remarked to Ford later, as he drove the hay truck across the bridge over the creek. "I think it's progress that they were connecting to their own animal, even if that did involve a fairly detailed discussion of horse poop."

Ford tilted his head. "Manure as a symbol of success. There's an interesting concept." But he gave her a grin.

They stopped at the fence gate and waited while Becky

and Lena jumped down from the truck bed to open the panel and let them through. When the girls had climbed on again, Ford eased the vehicle forward. "So they got the kitchen cleaned up?"

"They did. Dishes clean and dried and set out for breakfast tomorrow." Then she sighed. "That will be a challenge—waking them up early to cook a meal."

"Leave it to Garrett. He's about as irritating in the morning as a person can be. Cheerful, energetic, optimistic. It's disgusting."

She liked being able to watch him while he had to focus on the road. "You're not a morning person?"

"If morning starts about 9:00 a.m. With several cups of black coffee."

"Ranch work generally begins a lot earlier."

"It does. That's one of the perks of being an attorney."

Caroline shifted her weight on the seat. Just what she didn't want to hear about—why he stayed away.

"What about you?" Ford glanced at her. "An early riser?"

"'Fraid so. I'm up with the birds, and I crash shortly after sundown." She tried to shift the subject away from their differences. "Where exactly are we going?" she asked. "All the way to the mountains?"

The Big Horns were getting closer and higher, but Ford shook his head. "It's a rocky place on the bank of the creek, just right for sitting out with a fire. We called it our fort when Dylan was young, and the name kinda stuck. I haven't been there in probably five years."

"I guess life in San Francisco is just too exciting to get away very often." Caroline bit her lip. She hadn't meant to sound so bitchy.

He didn't seem to notice. "I don't know about exciting. I work a lot."

"No long weekends?" She couldn't seem to leave the subject alone. "Exotic vacations?"

"This summer is using up my vacations for the foreseeable future. I can't say when I'll get away next."

"You must really love your job."

"I'd better. I worked long and hard to get there."

"Of course." She angled her shoulders toward the window so she could blame the wind for her watery eyes. "Your family and—and the ranch will just wait till you can spare some time for them, I guess."

"That's what I count on."

Which made her feel terrible, because he sounded lonely and sad. She turned back to him, even reached out a hand to touch his shoulder.

But at that moment, Ford pulled the truck off the road they were following and onto a rough and rutted track heading into the trees. There were shouts and squeals from the truck bed as the kids got bounced around on their hay bales. Caroline braced herself against the door as they drove slowly into the wilderness.

They came to a clearing and stopped. "Welcome to Fort Marshall," Ford said. "Let the fun begin."

Chapter Seven

The kids were already out and about, exploring the area. Crazy Woman Creek rushed and tumbled along its rocky bed, framed by small trees and shrubs growing up between the stones. A plateau of giant, water-worn boulders created the perfect setting for a fire circle, with the clear sky above and plenty of room for sitting close to the firelight or retreating into the shadows.

"This is gorgeous." Caroline brought a load of firewood to the circle. "What a great place to have growing up."

"Wyatt found it," Ford said, setting logs into a teepee shape over a pile of small sticks and kindling. "Even Mr. MacPherson didn't know about it."

The forest formed a dense barrier around the clearing, but Marcos and Thomas were challenging the boundaries, walking a short way into the woods and then coming out again. Lena and Justino stood on a small sandy beach by the creek, holding hands and gazing at each other instead of the scenery.

Becky and Lizzie huddled close to where Ford worked.

"Are there bears?" Lizzie asked Caroline, glancing nervously around the clearing. "What will happen if we bother a bear?"

Ford answered the question. "I've never seen a bear here. Anyway, we're making too much noise—the bears will stay away." He smiled at her. "Try not to worry. We'll keep you safe."

His kindness wrung something in Caroline's chest, and she had to turn away so her reaction wouldn't be obvious. That brought Nate into her line of vision. He sat on a fallen tree at the far edge of the clearing, his elbows propped on his knees and his head down, obviously not enjoying his current surroundings.

She made her way over and sat down a little farther along the log. "Are you okay?"

He didn't look at her, but he nodded.

"You seem to be working on a problem. Is there something I can do?"

"No. Thanks."

"The fire is getting started. Want to come over and roast a marshmallow?"

"In a minute."

Caroline guessed that he was worried about his mother and sister. She regretted that Susannah Bradley wouldn't leave her abusive husband, for Nate's sake and her own. At least getting the boy out was a start—he could consider options for his life that might not seem possible when he was caught up in the violence at home.

"I'll be waiting for you to join us," she said, putting a hand on his shoulder before she walked back to the fire.

Although it had still been daylight when they left the ranch house, the setting sun had fallen behind the trees, and twilight now made the fire's brightness a welcome comfort. The kids came away from the edges of the clearing to sit on rocks still warm from the day. Even Lizzie started to relax, and was laughing as she leaned forward with her skewered marshmallow near the flames.

"And now," Dylan said, walking toward them from the truck, "the moment we've all been waiting for. Especially after that great demo this morning at the barn." He held up the guitar case he was carrying. "Anybody play?"

"Not me." Garrett stood by a small folding table, dispensing chocolate bars and graham crackers for s'mores. "Two left thumbs."

The kids shrugged or shook their heads. "We need a boombox," Marcos said loudly. "Get some real tunes going."

"We can do that one night," Caroline said, struck by inspiration. "We'll have a dance party, and you can choose the music."

"Oh, yeah," Justino said. Thomas started swaying to an imaginary beat.

"Meanwhile…" Dylan walked over to Ford. "We do have somebody who knows his way around a guitar. Bend those strings, bro."

With one eyebrow cocked, Ford glanced up at his youngest brother. "A little warning next time?" But he took the case, opened it and brought out the instrument. "Give me a minute to get tuned. This thing hasn't been played in forever."

As he plucked the different notes, an owl hooted from the woods nearby.

Lizzie jumped. "What was that?"

Thomas snorted. "Don't you recognize an owl call?"

"Is it going to attack us?"

"Might," Thomas said. "They are birds of prey."

Lizzie squealed and grabbed Becky by the shoulders.

"No," Caroline said firmly. "Nothing is going to attack us. Stop teasing, Thomas."

Ford struck a chord from the guitar. "So what can you guys sing? 'Row, Row Row Your Boat'?"

The kids groaned. "That's for babies," Thomas called out.

"Or grumpy old folks," Marcos added. "We want hip tunes, man."

"Real music," Justino added.

Ford stayed calm. "Such as?"

Lizzie raised her hand. "April Lowe sings cool songs." Caroline recognized the name of a popular young singer. Becky nodded vigorously.

"Hmm." Ford bent his head over the guitar and picked a few notes.

"That's right," Lizzie said. "That's her first big hit." She started singing lyrics about first love. The music filled in around the words, and Becky joined in. The two girls and Ford finished the song and two more before Marcos got restless.

"Come on, can't you play something real? Something with teeth?"

Ford grinned at him. "There's the one from this morning…" With a few chords he got Thomas and Marcos up on their feet, moving to the rap beat, imitating the voice of the singers they followed. Dylan picked up a couple of sticks and added percussion to the sound. Caroline noted that even Nate had come close enough to be seen in the firelight, though he didn't open his mouth to sing.

On the other hand, Justino and Lena were only visible from the knees down, as they sat on the edge of the circle. When another song started up, Caroline walked around to where the two had reclined into the darkness, kissing.

She toed Lena's hip and cleared her throat. "Not acceptable. This behavior belongs somewhere private."

They separated, and Justino sat up. "We don't get to be alone. What're we supposed to do?"

"Grow up a little," she told him, frustrated with the two kids and with her own reactions. "Or else one of you is going home."

Instead of rejoining the fire circle, she wandered around the clearing, listening to the music from a distance. Campfires were a romantic setting, and she could understand

Justino and Lena taking advantage of the situation. But she was really uncomfortable with how needy she was feeling.

What do you want? she asked herself. *To be a horny teenager again?*

Not at all. She wanted to be an adult woman with a man of her own—Ford Marshall, to be exact. To sit beside the fire with him, hold hands and kiss, to lie down and let him take her in his arms. To put her own arms around his strong shoulders and give to him all the passion she'd never offered to anyone else.

Instead, he would be leaving—he'd made that clear. His job would always win. Measured against the money and prestige he was used to, Caroline didn't stand a chance.

She came back to the campfire as Ford finally persuaded the kids to sing "On Top of Spaghetti," one of the least romantic campfire songs in the repertoire. Joining in, she tried to block notions of Ford the man—the lover—out of her mind.

They continued to sing until the stars shone bright in the black circle of sky above them, and until even Lizzie had relaxed.

"One more tune," Ford said. The fire had burned down, and their faces around it glowed red instead of gold. "Sing with me if you recognize it." And he started "Home on the Range."

If the kids knew the words, they weren't joining in. Everybody listened as Ford sang alone, his beautiful baritone voice a perfect frame for the melody. "'Then I would not exchange my home on the range, where the deer and the antelope play, where seldom is heard a discouraging word and the skies are not cloudy all day.'"

After he finished, the silence lasted for a long time. Dylan sat staring up at the sky, his face effectively hidden. Caroline gazed at Ford, but couldn't read his expression. Did he hear the longing in his own voice?

A log fell apart on the fire, and the moment broke. Garrett cleared his throat. "We should be heading toward the bunkhouse. We have an early call for breakfast tomorrow morning." Predictable complaints emerged from the teenagers.

"How are we supposed to find the truck in the dark?" Thomas sounded nervous. "I can't see nothing out here."

"That's why we have…ta-da…flashlights." Dylan raked the kids' faces with a bright white beam. "One for everybody—here you go."

In a matter of minutes—but with the maximum amount of light displays from the different torches—the fire was cold and wet, and the kids settled on their hay bales in the bed of the truck. Caroline suggested that Lizzie and Becky could ride in the cab with Ford, while she sat in the rear. Her emotions simmered too close to the surface to risk being alone with him again tonight.

And this was only the end of the first day.

ON THE RIDE from the fire circle to the ranch, Nate came up with a plan. He had to find out if things were okay at home. Calling wouldn't do any good—if his dad answered, he wouldn't admit anything was wrong. And Nate's mother wouldn't tell him the truth because she wanted him to stay at the ranch and "have fun."

The only way to know for sure was to be there. No one here would drive him into town, of course. They'd reassure him and send him off to bed like a little kid. How could he sleep, though, unless he was certain his mom and Amber were okay?

He remembered Miss Caroline saying it was about five miles from the Circle M Ranch to Bisons Creek. It would be a long run, but as a member of the track team at school, he'd gone farther. He went running most days, five to seven miles, as a way to work off steam. At least it would be cooler in the middle of the night.

All he had to do was wait till people fell asleep and then sneak out. Lucky thing he'd picked a bottom bunk, near the door. Nobody would miss him. He could be back in three hours, a long time before the sun rose and everyone else woke up.

No one would ever know.

FRESH AIR AND the day's excitement worked magic on the teenagers—once returned to the barn, only token protests erupted before the guys trailed off to the bunkhouse and the girls stumbled over to their cabin. From all appearances, they would be asleep in minutes.

Ford didn't believe it. "That was way too easy."

"Kids do get tired." Garrett pressed his fingers against his closed eyes. "Me, too."

Dylan nodded. "It's been a long day. But I want to spend a couple hours in the studio. Can I be excused from bed check?"

Garrett gave him a pat on the back. "Yeah. I'll be the bad guy. Catch you bright and early."

"Early, maybe. Bright is debatable." He headed toward the ranch house but then detoured just past the girls' cabin and headed for the old barn he used as a sculpture workshop.

"Will he really work tonight?" Caroline sounded worried. "He won't get much sleep."

"Dylan has always been a night owl," Garrett explained. "He gets by on four or five hours of sleep most nights."

"Until it catches up with him," Ford added. "Then he crashes and sleeps the clock round. Makes scheduling chores a little unpredictable."

Garrett frowned. "Not everybody works a nine-to-five job, Ford."

"And I do? I'll try telling my partners that when paperwork keeps me at the office till midnight."

"At least you can count it as billable hours. Some people don't get paid for overtime."

Ford clenched his jaw. "Those billable hours come in handy when the irrigation system breaks down or the tractor falls apart."

"This is just what we don't need, the two of you arguing." Caroline glared at them. "You're as grouchy as the kids. Why don't you go to your separate corners and come out tomorrow morning with a decent attitude? I am going to bed." With a flip of her ponytail, she stalked toward the cabin, the square set of her shoulders fending off any attempt to call her back.

Garrett blew out a breath. "Guess she told us."

Ford took off his hat and ran a hand through his hair. "Yeah." He hated to accept his own fatigue. His computer waited at the house with a day's worth of emails to be sorted. "Go on to bed. I'll make sure the boys have settled down."

"I'm wondering if I should bunk in with them." Garrett's shoulders slumped a little at the idea. "No telling what they'll get up to if they're left alone."

Ford shook his head. "I will probably regret saying this, but let's give them the benefit of the doubt. The keys to the vehicles are in the house, and we're five miles from anywhere they might want to be. The worst they can do is make a mess in the kitchen. Go on to bed."

"Thanks."

Ford watched his brother amble down toward the house before heading for the bunkhouse and whatever battle might lie ahead.

A kitchen light had been left burning and the television was on, but Marcos lay stretched out on the sofa, snoring softly. He'd flopped down in his clothes, without a pillow or a blanket. Grinning, Ford went to the closet and found a quilt to throw over the boy—nights on the range could get a little chilly.

In the bedroom, no one stirred as he opened the door, letting light from the kitchen pierce the darkness. He counted three bodies in three beds. So far, so good. Turning off the television, Ford said a quiet, "'Night, boys," and let himself out into the cool night air.

One day down. More than he wanted to think about left to go.

He'd been aware of Caroline all day, his gaze somehow finding her no matter where they or what they were doing. He was amazed at her patience and compassion for these kids—he probably would have packed them all into the van and sent them home after lunch. Definitely after the fiasco with the horses.

But Caroline had kept trying. She'd guided three of them through cooking dinner and handled the rough ones well enough to get the kitchen cleaned up. She'd led the singing around the campfire, catching one kid's glance and then another's—connecting, encouraging, making them feel part of the group. He'd noticed her talking with Nate, and whatever she'd said must have pulled him out of his shell enough to bring him to the fire circle, too. And she'd kept an eye on Justino and Lena. How did she manage to be aware of everything and everyone?

When all he could think about was her?

He'd let his temper get the best of him with Garrett, because of Caroline. Well, and because Garrett could be a little self-righteous sometimes. But mostly because Garrett had put his arm around Caroline's shoulders to give her a hug.

Of course, Ford wasn't sure he'd be able to stop with just a hug. He wanted so much more.

Taking a deep breath, he started down the hill, with a glance at the girls' cabin as he went.

Someone was sitting on the porch. He didn't have to squint to see who—he apparently had radar as far as she was concerned. Caroline.

Against his better judgment, but in line with all his inclinations, he walked up the hill to the cabin. The railing for the porch was at chest height, and he propped his arms on it.

"What are you doing out in the dark?"

She'd taken her hair down, and it curled around her face and shoulders in dark waves. "I wasn't quite ready to fall asleep. I wanted to sit outside and unwind a little."

"I'm disturbing you. Sorry." Ford started to turn away.

"Not at all." The words were a little rushed. "I mean… you're welcome to stay. It's—it's a nice night."

"Yeah." Now that he'd come over, he had no idea what to say. "The campfire went pretty well. No major disasters."

"I was proud of them. You'd think they were just innocent kids, having a good time."

"That's the trouble, isn't it? They're kids, but they're not innocent."

"Yes, that's the trouble. In some way or another, their world has broken down and left them trying to cope, when they're not experienced enough to handle their situations."

"Do you really believe being here will make a difference?"

She gazed at him for a minute in silence. "I have to try."

He couldn't let it go. "Why? Why does a woman with your background and resources give it all up to work this damned hard?" She didn't say anything for so long, he figured she wasn't going to. "Never mind. Blame me for being a lawyer—we ask nosy questions."

"It's okay." She took a breath. "I always hesitate to re-visit it. But you deserve an answer, since I've involved you in this effort. You were right—I *was* pretty spoiled when I graduated from high school. And I took that sense of entitlement to college with me. Rode for the rodeo team, skimmed through my classes, lived it up. My roommate, Dena, was a barrel racer, too. We became close friends, even though we were competing against each other."

Another deep breath. "Dena came from the real world, the one I hadn't seen much of till then. Her dad had run off, her mom worked two jobs and Dena herself started cleaning stalls at a nearby ranch when she was barely thir-teen. That's where she learned to ride and she just hap-pened to be very talented. But she also partied pretty hard with a tough crowd. I tried to talk to her, but she would complain that I was being a princess and blow me off." Caroline's gaze met his. "Eventually, I realized she was doing drugs. By junior year, she was always either high or crashing—never just herself anymore. Finally, she got kicked off the rodeo team. Stopped going to classes, was being threatened with expulsion."

Caroline covered her face with her hands for a mo-ment. "Before that could happen, she overdosed. I found her in our room, covered with—" She choked then went on. "Dena didn't die, fortunately. But she's a ghost—brain damaged, emotionally empty… She'll never be the bright, happy girl who was my friend."

Ford propped his chin on his hands. "You're still try-ing to save Dena?"

"I'm trying to keep as many kids as I can from going down that path. Hoping to rescue the ones already at risk. I guess that seems like a pretty futile effort, but—"

He held up a hand to stop her. In the quiet night, he had heard a noise that seemed out of place. A thunk.

"What is it?"

"A door closing."

She gave him a puzzled look.

"The back door to this place."

"Lena?"

"That would be my guess. Go check her bed. I'll meet you at the barn."

Ford waited until she joined him at the barn door. "If it were me, I'd head for the sofa in the tack room," he said in a low voice.

"Lead the way," she told him, and her hand found his with a firm clasp.

Even after years away, he knew the barn as well as his own face, and he navigated easily past the stalls and the tools to the rear of the building. No lights had been turned on, but he could hear whispers and giggles, and he figured the tack room door must be ajar. Quietly, he snaked his arm through the opening and found the light switch. He gave Caroline's fingers a squeeze and let go.

Then he flipped the switch.

Lena screamed. Justino swore. Ford pushed the door open so that Caroline could enter the room. The teenagers cowered on the couch. Shirts were already unbuttoned.

"Give me one reason," Caroline said, when the noise quieted down, "why I shouldn't send Lena home. One good reason."

"Please," the girl said through her tears. "I'll have to spend the whole summer taking care of my brothers. Cooking, cleaning. Since my mom…died…my dad makes me responsible for everything. I work all the time at home."

"He makes her do all the housework, the laundry." Justino put his arm around Lena. "She falls asleep in class because she gets no rest at home. They're little boys. But she's not their mother."

Ford felt Caroline soften beside him. "That's tough,"

she said. "But I can't have you two meeting this way. I wouldn't be fulfilling my responsibility to your parents if I didn't supervise you. And—I'm going to be really honest here—I don't want Lena to end up pregnant this summer. That's where you're headed with this behavior. So what are we going to do?"

Lena had buttoned her shirt, and now she stood up. "We'll do better, honest. We'll stick to the rules."

Justino got to his feet more slowly, his shirt still hanging open. He was a handsome young man on the cusp of maturity, and Ford understood too well the urges driving him.

Caroline didn't let him off the hook. "Justino?"

"Sure," the boy said, but didn't meet Ford's eyes. "I'll do whatever Lena says."

"Both of you get to bed. Now. You should be exhausted, and I certainly am."

Ford flipped on a light in the barn, closed up the tack room, and then he and Caroline followed the teenagers out. Lena and Justino shared a longing gaze and a defiant kiss before separating. Two slams announced their return to their sleeping quarters.

"Whew." Shaking her head, Caroline started toward the cabin. "That was tough."

Ford walked beside her. "Do you believe they'll obey the rules?"

"They'll try, for a day or two."

"We could lock them in."

"It's an idea." She smiled at him. "But what would that teach them?"

"Don't mess with adults?"

"Don't get caught, is more likely."

They reached the steps of the cabin. Caroline climbed the first step and then pivoted to face him. "I'm glad you were there. I appreciated having your support for that confrontation. And Justino will listen better to a man than to me."

"I didn't say anything." The step brought their heads level, so his eyes could meet hers, a shining green even in the dark. Her tousled hair looked so soft, his fingers actually twitched with the desire to touch it.

"You were on my side," she insisted. Then she blew a breath off her full lower lip. "I'd better get in. It's late."

"Yeah." But neither of them moved. Being this close to her felt right to Ford, the way the day should end, with the two of them sharing thoughts and feelings. So kissing Caroline was the only natural evolution of the moment. Her soft mouth tilted slightly against his, her lips parted and her warm breath whispered over his cheek. He put an arm around her waist and a hand to her hair, threading his fingers through that dusky softness. She seemed small in his hold, but not weak, especially when her arms locked around his neck, and she pressed closer against him with a demand he had to answer. He braced one foot on the step beside her and tightened his hold, pressing their bodies together from knee to chest, the roundness of her breasts a sensuous fullness against him, her belly an erotic pressure between his legs.

Their kisses went wild, crazy and devouring. Ford tasted her tongue, the ridges of her teeth, the smooth warmth of her mouth. Breaking free, he roamed his lips along the curve of her neck to the open throat of her shirt and the pulse pounding there. He laid his hands below her waist, cupped her bottom and pulled her even closer against him, against the ache she'd stirred that lived within him night and day.

"Ford. Ford, please." Caroline was kissing his forehead, running her hands through his hair, over his shoulders and spine.

He understood what she wanted. Breathing hard, struggling to assert control over himself and his desire, he managed to loosen his hands and put some distance between them. With a deep breath he stepped away, turning his back to her, grinding the heels of his hands against his burning eyes.

"Sorry," he muttered. "I didn't mean…to get out of hand."

"Me, too." Her voice shook. "My fault as much as yours."

He cleared his throat. "I won't let it happen again."

"We can't—" she said at the same moment. "The kids…"

"Sure. And Garrett."

"And Dylan," Caroline added. "Wyatt, too."

"Right." He didn't trust himself to face her, to see her standing in the moonlight. "Go on in. I'll wait till the door shuts."

He heard her boots cross the porch. There was a long silence.

"'Night," she said, finally.

Ford just nodded. The door squeaked open, shut firmly. The porch light went out.

Alone in the dark, Ford stared up at the stars, sprinkled like glitter across the black velvet sky. So far, this week was proceeding as badly as he'd predicted, especially when it came to Caroline. Even the presence of seven teenagers and his brothers couldn't stifle his need for her. She hadn't kissed him as if Garrett was an issue between them. But he hadn't kissed her with the restraint of a man who would be leaving in a matter of weeks, either. What could they do with this inconvenient, compelling passion? How would they manage the rest of the summer?

And what about the rest of their lives?

Chapter Eight

With his breath almost normal, Nate hurried past the ranch house, using the cover of the trucks parked out front to screen him from the windows. It was a little after 4:00 a.m., but somebody might be up already. Or be having trouble sleeping. And he for sure didn't want to be seen.

At the bunkhouse, he took off his sneakers and silently slipped past the door. He would have loved a glass of water after his run, but that would make noise. He'd have to wait till morning.

He could relax now, anyway, because his mom had said his dad would be staying at the Donnelly Ranch during the week for his new job. Maybe, having a job, he wouldn't be drinking so much on the weekends, and things would settle down. They could always hope.

Of course, she'd yelled at him, too, for leaving the ranch and going home. She'd made him promise not to do it again. And she hadn't let him run all the way back, but had loaded a sleeping Amber in the car and driven him to the ranch entrance. The jog from there had been easy. Now he could slide into bed—

"Well, well. What's happenin', dude?"

The lamp beside the sofa came on. Nate jerked around to see Marcos sitting up. "Nothing," Nate said. "Just went for a walk. Couldn't sleep."

"Pretty long walk. You left about three hours ago. Where ya been?"

"Around." He swallowed against his pounding heartbeat. "Watching the horses."

Marcos went to the bathroom, peed without shutting the door and then came into the living room again. "I don't think so. You met one of the girls, right? You and Lizzie, doin' it in the barn?"

Nate frowned. "No. Just forget it, Marcos. Go to sleep." He headed toward the bedroom door, trying to bluff his way through this.

But Marcos wrapped a hand around his arm and jerked him around. "Hold on, dude. I bet the fools running this place would be interested in finding out that you were wandering around in the middle of the night."

"Come on, Marcos. Leave me alone. I'm not bothering you."

"You bother me by just breathing, dude. What are we gonna do about it?"

Nate blew out a breath. He didn't remember a time when he wasn't being bullied by somebody. His dad was the worst. "What do you want?"

"Good question. Let's see…what do I want?" He pretended to consider, rubbing his chin with his fingers. "I want these losers to stop bugging me about cooking and cleaning."

"I can't do anything about that."

"Sure you can. You can take my place."

Nate stared at him. "You don't think they might notice I'm not you?"

"As long as they got the right number of slaves, they won't care. So from now on, you show up to do my job. I'll keep my mouth shut about your little adventures as long as you do."

"Your name's on the chart." Nate tilted his head toward the bulletin board. "They read, you know."

"I'll take care of it. You just do the work." Marcos shoved him forward into a stumble. "Hit the sack, dude. You gotta get up and cook breakfast."

"Whatever." Picking up the shoes he'd dropped, Nate eased through the door to the bedroom and shut it behind him. Justino and Thomas hadn't moved, as far as he could tell. He crawled under the covers of his own bunk and lay there breathing hard, his body aching with exertion and pure fatigue. Marcos's plan wouldn't work, so he wasn't going to worry about it. If it did work, so what? There were worse problems than having to cook three times a day.

Like watching your dad beat up your mom and not being able to stop him.

CAROLINE HAD NO trouble waking up early. At six o'clock, she was already lying with her eyes wide open, thinking about Ford. Having no hope for further sleep, she rolled out of bed, showered and dressed. At least she didn't have to wait for three teenage girls to finish in the bathroom.

Out on the porch, she sat in the same rocking chair she'd occupied last night, shivering a little in the chilly dawn air. She stared at the ranch house down the hill and wondered which room belonged to Ford. Was he already awake? Had he slept as badly as she had?

At seven she went into the house to wake the girls. Ford and Dylan had moved an extra single bed into the largest bedroom, where there was already a double, so all three girls could share the space.

Standing in the doorway, Caroline knocked on the wall. "Rise and shine, girls. Breakfast in thirty minutes."

In the single bed, Lena didn't move a muscle. Becky groaned and rolled over, disturbing Lizzie next to her.

"No," Lizzie moaned. "I'm not hungry."

"You will be by ten o'clock, unless you eat now. Come on, kids. You can do it." Caroline stepped over to shake Lena's shoulder. "Wake up, Lena. Time to get going. We've got three people here who will want the bathroom."

Lena muttered something in Spanish that Caroline was pretty sure she didn't want to translate. "This is stupid. I need more sleep."

"Maybe you should get to bed earlier."

The girl opened one eye and glared at Caroline. She understood the message. But she didn't like it.

"I'm going over to get the guys cooking. We will start eating at seven thirty. I'll send Ford to get you if you're not there."

With that threat, she left the house and headed for the bunkhouse, where Garrett was supposed to have gotten the boys up and moving. That was the plan, anyway.

Instead, all four boys were still asleep, as still as if they hadn't moved a muscle all night.

Caroline stood motionless for a minute, hands fisted at her sides. Was she the only responsible adult on the premises? She might as well be running the entire project by herself.

Then she took a deep breath, relaxed her hands and loosened her stiff shoulders. Garrett and Dylan meant well, and they'd been a big help. Maybe she'd forgotten to ask Garrett to wake the boys. The mix-up could be her fault.

And Ford…Ford had been with her last night when she'd confronted Justino and Lena. Whenever there was trouble, he seemed to be there to help her solve the problem. She couldn't really imagine how she'd be handling these kids without him.

Behind her, the outside door opened. She turned and was somehow not surprised when Ford stepped inside.

"'Morning," he said, in a gravelly voice. "These guys still asleep?"

She nodded as he crossed the room. "Wasn't Garrett supposed to get them up?"

He thought a second. "I said he could, but I don't believe we gave him that task specifically." His eyes looked tired, his face a little pale. It seemed he hadn't slept well, either.

"My mistake. Well, it's past time they were out of bed." She started toward the bedroom.

Ford caught her arm. "Let me. You wait over in the kitchen. Or even better, at the house. Garrett's got coffee brewed."

"You're sure?"

"Yes. Show up at seven thirty and breakfast will be underway."

"Great." Such a relief, to be able to count on him to handle the boys. "Thanks so much."

"No problem. Now go." He gave her a little push from behind. "Vamoose."

She checked on the girls again—they were moving slowly, but at least they were moving. So she went down to the ranch house and found Garrett in the kitchen alone.

"Good morning," he said cheerfully. "Coffee? You take cream and sugar, right?"

She sipped from the mug he handed her and sighed. "Just right. You're a genius with the java."

"That makes one thing I'm a genius with. Are the boys up?"

"Um…probably. Ford's over there."

"Of course he is. He's the world's best organizer."

"He mentioned that you're an early riser, really energetic in the mornings."

"Usually. It's a chance for a fresh start, after the mistakes of yesterday."

"True. And since you're so motivated in the morning, can I put you in charge of getting the guys up? They ought to be dressed before the girls come over to cook, when they aren't doing the cooking. Anyway, they ought to be up at seven."

"Sure, I'll be glad to. Ford should have sent me over today, instead of going himself." Garrett shook his head. "He doesn't delegate very well, just gets it done and moves on to the next task."

"He's easy to depend on."

Wyatt spoke from the kitchen doorway. "He takes on a lot of responsibility he doesn't necessarily have to." He walked stiffly to the counter and poured himself a mug. "We could have managed this summer without him."

Garrett started setting up a fresh pot. "I'm not sure we could have helped Caroline with the kids if Ford hadn't been here. They're a big commitment."

"True. And I'm glad he's home for a while. Too bad we can't convince him to stay."

Caroline couldn't resist asking, "He loves his job in San Francisco so much?"

Garrett and Wyatt looked at each other. "I…I don't know about that," Wyatt said, finally. "He's talented and sharp at what he does. He takes pride in his work. Mostly, though, I think he feels compelled to bring in a hefty paycheck. Considers it his responsibility to the family and the ranch."

The truth struck her hard. Ford's commitment to his brothers kept him working in San Francisco, at the big law firm, earning big money. For him to relocate to Bisons Creek permanently would mean abdicating his duty to the family, something a Marshall boy—especially Ford—would never do. And she wouldn't ask him to.

Walking up to the cabin with a fresh mug of coffee, Caroline resolved to keep her interactions with Ford strictly casual. She needed to maintain distance between them physically but also emotionally, which would be harder. Just because he was the most honorable and charismatic man she'd ever met did not mean that they were meant to be together.

She was perfectly happy being single. For the rest of her life.

ROUSTING TEENAGE BOYS at 7:00 a.m. was similar to waking up cowhands who had tied one on the night before. Extra effort was required, along with a high tolerance for insults.

Even Nathan, who usually did what was asked right away, resisted getting up. Ford abandoned the cold washcloth he'd used on Justino and Thomas, but he finally had to strip the covers off, leaving Nate shivering in his pajamas.

"You'll want to be dressed before the girls come in," he told the boy. "That gives you about five minutes."

Nate struggled to sit up on the side of the bunk, but he still appeared half-dead.

"Are you sick?" Ford scrutinized him more carefully. "Should I take your temperature?"

"I'm okay," he said, in a barely audible voice. "Just tired."

"Sorry." Ford softened his tone. "I suspect we can all say that. Maybe we'll schedule a group nap for this afternoon."

The corners of Nate's mouth lifted slightly. "Sounds good."

By the time the four boys were dressed, seven thirty had long passed. The girls walked in at eight, followed by Caroline, looking a little frustrated.

She became even more so when she caught sight of the breakfast table. "Cereal? The menu says—"

Ford put up a hand to stop her. "Eggs and bacon just

weren't happening this morning. The cooks were slow getting started, and there were some…uh…objections to the process. We decided to serve something simple so everybody could eat and keep the day on schedule."

Caroline surveyed Thomas, Marcos and Justino, who were standing in the kitchen. Their attempts at nonchalance couldn't disguise the underlying nervousness.

She nodded once. "Got it. Sometimes the day just starts off hard, doesn't it? But cereal and fruit works, so let's all sit down and get something to eat."

The kids didn't wait for a second invitation. Chairs scraped as each one found the seat they'd chosen as theirs, and the sound of cornflakes hitting the bottom of the bowl took over. Ford watched from the kitchen area as everybody settled down to their food with enthusiasm.

Caroline joined him. "Does that mean Marcos refused to cook?"

"As a matter of fact, yes."

"Which set the other two off, as well."

Ford nodded. "Full-scale rebellion."

"You worked a miracle, then, getting them to set out any food at all."

"I have to confess that I did remind them that they wouldn't eat if they didn't do the work."

"Brute force does it again."

"They are teenage boys."

Caroline took a deep breath. "I guess we should anticipate the same problem at dinner. Overcoming this macho mind-set is getting to be a challenge."

"You've got burgers on the menu. We'll haul the grill over here and let them cook outside. Maybe that will seem more manly."

"Brilliant!" She grinned at him, her eyes sparkling, and he couldn't help smiling in response.

But in the next instant, her liveliness snapped off like

a blown lightbulb. Her face now a blank mask, Caroline resumed watching the kids. "If we're lucky, that approach will ease them into cooking mode. Thanks for coming up with it." She walked over to the table, sat down in an empty chair next to Becky and went about getting her own breakfast.

Ford stayed where he was. He understood what had happened, as surely as if a flashing neon sign hung over Caroline's head saying Second Thoughts. She must have reconsidered, as he had last night, and come to the same conclusion—the farther apart they stayed, the better for everyone.

The hollow inside him got a little bigger with the knowledge.

In a few minutes, the noise level started to climb, a sure indicator that the kids were finished with their meal. Caroline stood up and clapped her hands to get their attention. "Clean up this morning is assigned to Lizzie, Lena and Nate. The cooks can go with Ford to bring the horses in. We'll all meet in front of the barn at nine."

The grumbling began on two fronts, as Lizzie and Lena complained about doing dishes while Marcos complained about having to do anything at all. Thomas and Justino stayed in their seats, pushing their dishes down the table toward Nate, who walked them over to the sink. Caroline took on the girls, steering Lizzie and Lena to their tasks. That left Ford to handle the guys. Again.

He put one hand on Thomas's shoulder and one on Justino's. "Outside," he said. "That's where the horses are." He went to confront Marcos, who had retreated to the sofa. "Spending the day in bed?"

The boy grinned. "Sounds sweet, huh? I could get into that." He started to swing his feet up to lie down. But Ford grabbed his ankles

"Hey! Let go!"

Ford dropped his feet on the floor. "We've got things to do, Marcos. Outside."

"Keep your hands off me." Flushed and breathing hard, Marcos came to his feet with just inches between his face and Ford's. "You ain't my old man."

The difference in their heights was about six inches, which made the challenge a little ridiculous. But Ford didn't laugh. "You'd be sorry if I was. Now get outside."

Marcos did his best to be intimidating. The fierce stare, the puffed chest and clenched fists might have worked with other kids, maybe with teachers.

Ford spun on his heel and walked away, leaving the bunkhouse. He found Thomas and Justino kicking rocks around in the road as they headed to the barn and watched them for about a minute…until Marcos came out of the building.

"Great." Ford nodded but didn't wait for an explanation or apology. "Let's go gather the horses."

As they approached the barn, Thomas said, "We gotta go catch all those horses? Man, I can't see that happening."

"It's not as hard as you might imagine." Ford led them through the barn and out into the corral. "First, check to be sure the gate by the barn is closed. Make certain the doors to the barn are fastened, too. Now, follow me."

He led them to the gate between the corral and the pasture, opened it and swung it wide, against the fence. "What we want to do is drive the horses toward this end of the pasture and into the corral through this gate."

Justino rubbed his hand over his head. "How?"

"Walk beyond them, and then come back toward this end. You can wave your arms, say 'Shoo' or 'Go on,' something to get them moving one way or the other. Your job, once they're moving, is to keep them going this way and to make sure they don't go farther out. Got it?"

"Not really." Thomas stood with his hands on his hips.

"I don't understand why they'd move when they got all the grass they can eat out there."

"You'll figure it out." Ford went through the gate. "Try just walking up to your horse. Or any horse. See what happens."

He watched from a distance as the boys moved toward the nearest animals. Predictably, when each boy got within a certain distance, the horse would shift to a different patch of grass. After three such encounters, Marcos glanced around.

"It keeps moving away. This is stupid."

"Where are you supposed to go?"

"Beyond," Thomas said. "You mean we can get them to move away from us but toward the pen?"

"That's the plan."

Thomas gazed toward the more distant horses. "They're a long way off."

"Better get walking."

He rolled his eyes. "Man." But he headed toward the outliers. After a minute, Justino followed.

"Let's get to work, Marcos. You can move these three."

Marcos's first efforts weren't impressive, but as he figured out the method, his enthusiasm increased. The gamelike aspects of the process became apparent, and the exercise gave him a chance to stretch and run. Farther out, Thomas and Justino were having pretty good luck heading in the other members of the herd, and were clearly enjoying themselves doing it.

Maybe they weren't the fastest crew when it came to bringing in a string of horses, but Ford considered the activity a definite success.

"Great job, guys," he told them when the gate was closed and the horses were milling around the corral. "Let's go meet Caroline and report on the success you've already had this morning."

He had to smile at the cocky aspect to all three boys' walks as they went through the barn. But his own pleasure in their accomplishment was...disturbing. He had opposed this project. Getting attached to these kids—as troublesome as they were—would not be a smart idea.

Then again, how attached could he get in two weeks? He still couldn't imagine this situation lasting any longer, no matter how hard Caroline tried.

Out in front of the barn, Garrett was just pulling up in his truck, with a horse trailer attached. "We have a visitor," he announced, going around to open the rear door of the trailer. "Give me just a minute to get him out."

The kids were amazingly quiet as they waited, which telegraphed more interest in the process than they probably would have wanted anyone to realize. Caroline held the trailer door open, and glanced at them over her shoulder. "This is awesome."

Ford had seen his share of horses, large and small. But as Garrett led this one out of the trailer, he decided it just might be the cutest pony he'd ever laid eyes on. Mostly brown but with a black mane and lots of flashy white markings, he was a kind-looking horse with dark eyes and nothing at all about him to make anyone nervous. Even Lizzie.

"This is Major," Garrett announced. "We borrowed him from some neighbors to help you guys get accustomed to horses."

Becky and Lena approached right away, with Justino following. The girls stroked the glossy brown neck and face, talking to the pony as if he was a little kid. Thomas and Marcos moved closer, too, because the animal was just too appealing to ignore. Nate stood at the pony's middle, resting a hand on his ribs and appearing content, if not actually happy. The pony didn't seem bothered by all the people standing around and calmly accepted their attention.

"Hey, Lizzie," Becky called, "come check him out. He's really nice."

Lizzie stood huddled into herself, arms wrapped around her waist, her face white and drawn. Tension radiated from her body, and Ford thought she might bolt for the cabin at any second.

But she surprised him and stepped forward, moving toward the pony.

Size really did matter, Ford decided. Major was a good six inches shorter than Sundance, the chestnut Lizzie had worked with yesterday. And where Sundance held her head up high, even when relaxed, Major tended to keep his head low, which made him seem even smaller. As Lizzie got closer, she relaxed her arms, letting her hands fall to her sides. Becky moved away so her friend could reach the pony directly. Everybody seemed to be holding their breath as Lizzie put her fingers on Major's cheek.

"Hey, boy," she said. "Aren't you sweet?"

BY LUNCH CAROLINE felt totally justified to be optimistic about the kids and their progress. Lizzie's success with Major had encouraged all of them to develop a better relationship with their horses, and the morning had gone by without any tantrums from teenagers or animals. As a surprise, Dylan drove into town and returned with a stack of pizzas for lunch, which earned him all-around appreciation. After an hour of free time, everybody met at the corral for the afternoon's project—saddling a horse.

"Each horse has its own saddle," Ford explained, "because they all have different shapes, and the saddle must fit really well for the horse to be able to work." They were in the tack room of the barn, where most of the saddles were stored. "We'll make sure your saddle fits you pretty well, too. The stirrups—" he held one up, just in case somebody was confused "—get longer or shorter, depending on how long your legs are."

"We have to saddle our own horse?" Lena frowned.

"You'll get as much help as you need," Caroline said. "But the fact is, you should be sure the saddle is put on right, as a matter of safety. And the best way to confirm that is to do it yourself."

"I don't know nothin' about saddles. Leave it to me, I fall off." Marcos pretended he was tipping sideways off a horse, which made most of the kids laugh, and they started to imitate him.

Ford gave them a chance to fool around before continuing. "I've had that happen to me. One minute I'm sitting up tall, then the saddle starts sliding around till I'm pretty much hanging upside down. The horse is running off, and I'm getting hit in the face with grass."

"How old were you?" Thomas asked.

"About your age. We'd just started working here. Mr. MacPherson assumed we could ride, and I didn't want to confess the truth. I looked like an idiot."

He'd caught their attention again, giving them a story they could relate to. Caroline stood quiet as they asked Ford about his experience, silently reveling in the joy of having provided these at-risk kids with such a great role model.

And he'll make a great parent one day, she caught herself thinking. *Just not with me.*

She cleared her mind and then cleared her throat to get everybody's attention. "Okay, we'll take each one of you individually to help you put the saddle on your horse. Ford and Nate, Garrett and Becky, Dylan and Justino. I'll work with Lena. Let's go. The others can hang out on the couch for a while."

The first hurdle was, of course, just lifting the saddle

to carry it outside. None of the kids was prepared for the sheer weight of that much leather and wood. Justino managed to handle his own, but the girls couldn't. And Nate was struggling until Ford took over.

After putting on a saddle blanket, the real challenge became getting the saddle itself onto the horse's back, which was at shoulder height or higher for most of them.

"More cowboy weight lifting," Justino muttered, trying to throw the heavy saddle onto his horse and failing. "This is stupid."

Finally, with grown-up help, seven saddles were placed, the girths tightened and a bridle put on each horse. The adults would probably have to do most of the saddling this summer, as the kids just wouldn't develop enough muscle. But at least they'd be aware of what to do.

The bridles came off, the girths were undone, the saddle removed and replaced in the tack room. By that point the kids were sweaty, dusty and tired.

"I'm goin' home," Marcos said. "This is about as fun as gettin' detention. Hell, I'd rather get detention. Least it's air-conditioned."

"I'm with you, man." Thomas pulled his damp shirt away from his chest. "This sucks."

Caroline tried to take the grumbling in stride. "It will get easier. Give your horse a good brushing, then we'll turn them out and you can chill before dinner. We won't even make you move hay." She grinned at them but got only glares in response.

"More dirt." Justino coughed. "I never knew horses were this dirty." He spit into the dust at his feet. "I want a shower."

The girls complained less, but their silence was as much an indication of discontent as the boys' words. While Ford sent the herd of horses through the pasture gate, the seven bedraggled teens shuffled through to the front of the barn and divided toward their separate houses. Even Lena and Justino didn't linger.

"We pushed them pretty hard," Garrett said, frowning with worry. "Maybe we should slow down."

Dylan put his head down on a bale of hay. "We pushed *me* pretty hard. I'm beat."

"We're not done," Ford said as he joined them. "We're going to move the grill up so the guys can cook burgers for dinner. I can't lift it alone. Come on, Dylan. They'll be wanting to eat soon."

Garrett waved them on. "I'll supervise the cooking." He glanced at Caroline. "You okay?"

Caroline jumped. "What? Oh, sure." She'd been watching Ford walk away, admiring his clean stride and narrow hips. "I was thinking about tomorrow's riding lesson."

"Thinking about my brother is closer to the truth." He stared her down. "Right?"

"Um…" She wasn't ready to admit such a thing to one of Ford's brothers. Especially not to Garrett, the minister.

He put a hand on her shoulder. "I'm not blind, and you're exceptionally easy to read. You and Ford remind me of peacocks, circling around each other in a mating dance."

"Garrett! We do not."

"I don't object, you understand. Ford deserves a very special woman, and you definitely fit that description. You could be really happy together."

"But…"

"But I see you with these kids, with women like Susannah Bradley who need your support and refuge, and I want to keep you in Bisons Creek." He shrugged. "Ford will take you to San Francisco. And sure, there are a host of people there who could use your help just as much as we do, if not more." His cheeks reddened. "I'm being selfish, I guess. I want you here, with me. As a friend and a colleague."

"Oh, Garrett." On impulse, Caroline put her arms around his shoulders and gave him a hard hug. "You're so sweet. Believe me, I have no plans to leave. This is my home, and these are the people I...well, I feel called to work with." Drawing away, she kissed his cheek. "I promise."

"Glad to hear that." Garrett's worried expression evaporated. "I'll rest better knowing we can count on you for the long run." He thought for a second. "And who can tell? Maybe you'll be the reason Ford comes home."

"I don't—"

Before she could finish her protest, brakes squealed sharply nearby. Caroline jerked around to see a truck parked near the front of the bunkhouse.

Dylan got out of the passenger seat and looked back inside. "You must not drive much, bro," he said loudly, "the way you're using the brakes. Out here, we ease to a stop." At the rear of the truck, he let down the tailgate in front of the big gas grill in the bed. "Especially with kids running around."

The driver's door slammed, and Ford came around to join him. He grabbed the frame of the grill and pulled it toward him. "Ready?"

They set the grill on the ground and rolled it to a spot near the door. In just a few minutes the gas tank was attached and the top flipped up, inviting a barbecue. The kids stood around it, admiring the stainless-steel luxury.

Ford put the tailgate up and then glanced briefly toward the barn. "I've got to go into town," he called. His face was set in hard lines. "Should I pick up anything?"

He waited barely ten seconds before he was in the truck, slamming the door yet again. No one could criticize the care with which he reversed and turned, but as soon as he passed the ranch house, the truck engine roared, and the vehicle disappeared in a cloud of dust.

"What the hell," Garrett said, "was that all about?"

Chapter Nine

Hands tight on the steering wheel, Ford headed in the opposite direction from Bisons Creek, toward Kaycee and a dimly lit bar he'd stopped in occasionally over the years.

At the door, he noticed a poster tacked up at eye level on the wall for the "Kaycee Summer Rodeo," to be held this coming Saturday. "Bronc Riding, Bull Riding, Barrel Racing! Enter at the Gate! Barn Dance Follows!" the poster advertised.

That would be the rodeo Caroline had proposed taking the kids to for a weekend adventure. Maybe they'd witness what an experienced rider could do, she'd suggested, and be inspired with their own horses. At least they'd get away from the ranch for a little while.

But if let loose at the rodeo, could they all be rounded up again? How would Caroline and the Marshalls keep track of seven stubborn kids in that crowd? The possibilities for disaster were mind-boggling.

Inside the bar, Ford ducked into a booth but ordered only a cola. He didn't really want alcohol. He wanted Caroline. And seeing her with her arms around his brother had flayed him to the bone.

"You look like you've got a heap of troubles." The red-haired waitress set a glass in front of him. "Women, family or business?"

Ford choked a laugh. "How about all three?"

She whistled. "Which one bothers you the most?"

"That would be the problem. I don't know."

"Whew. Sure you don't want the hard stuff? Might help you decide."

He shook his head.

"Well, holler for a refill." She slapped the table with a green-nailed hand and sauntered away to put a coin in the juke box. "Your Cheatin' Heart" slipped into the air.

With half his drink gone, Ford sat back and rubbed his eyes. Playing hooky from the ranch wasn't going to solve his problems. Returning to San Francisco would, though. He'd get away from Caroline and an attraction he couldn't control, get away from the troublesome teenagers monopolizing his time and rejoin the uncomplicated life he'd built for himself.

That was what he wanted. Wasn't it?

He wasn't sure anymore. He couldn't see straight down the road he'd been following for so long. There were obstacles now, Caroline being the biggest one—a huge boulder blocking his way and making him consider taking an unexpected turn.

The teenagers drove him crazy, but they also challenged him, entertained him, even touched him on an uncomfortable level. Their unpredictable nature kept him alert in ways he wasn't sure he'd experienced for years.

Then there were his brothers…starting with Garrett, who might or might not be in love with Caroline, but who needed moral support as he dealt with the town, his church and the ranch. Dylan was just starting his career as an artist, but was struggling to find more time to do that work. Another hand on the ranch would make a big difference to both of them.

And he couldn't forget Wyatt, who had borne most of the burdens for almost twenty years now. Was ranching all he wanted for himself? Being tied every single day to a piece of land and a herd of cattle, making ends meet, making repairs, making do with what he had? What did he expect out of life, anyway?

Ford finished his drink and set the glass down slowly. Those were the questions. He had no idea what the answer to even a single one of them might be.

He slid out of the booth, leaving a five on the table.

The waitress stood behind the bar. "Got all those problems rounded up?"

"Nope. But I have an idea about where to start looking for the answers."

"Good for you, cowboy. You're halfway home."

I hope so. Ford climbed into the truck and headed for home. *Or else I'll be lost for good.*

THE DAY HAD BEEN warm and, after the dust of the corral, the shade of cottonwood trees over the trickle of cool water made a nice change. Marcos, Thomas and Justino had waded into the creek in their jeans, while the girls and Nate perched on rocks nearby. Caroline sat on a boulder at a distance from the splash zone, laughing at the boys' antics.

She jumped a little when Ford suddenly appeared beside her. "This was a great idea," he said. "They seem to be having fun. Finally."

After his disappearing act, she wasn't sure what to say to him. "It was Dylan's suggestion. He mentioned how much he loved playing in the creek."

Ford leaned against a nearby tree trunk, leaving plenty of space between them. "We called him 'Tadpole' during the summers. He was down here every chance he could sneak away."

She kept her gaze on the teenagers. "They pretend to be so tough, grown up. But they're really still children."

"You chose the right kids. Many teens would have been a problem in this situation."

She glanced his way. "You're thinking about someone specific?"

"I was a Big Brother in college to this boy named Lamont." He kept his eyes on the group in the creek, as well. "Fourteen, but small for his age. Jobless mother, no dad in sight, five younger siblings. The goal was simply to get him to stay in school."

Now she swiveled to face him. "What did you do?"

"Played ball with him, fed him, took him to movies and museums and sports events. Helped him with schoolwork, of course. Found his mother a job, which lasted for about a month, till she stopped showing up. Some nights, I fed the whole family, bathed his little brothers and put them to bed." He shrugged a shoulder. "I liked him a lot. He was clever, with a smart mouth. He could have done something big with his life."

But somehow it had gone wrong. "What happened?"

After a pause, Ford cleared his throat. "One night, I was coming home late from the library. I didn't live in a safe neighborhood—couldn't afford it. But that evening it was pretty quiet, the street was empty…until a guy stepped out of the alley and pulled a gun on me."

"Ford!"

"It was Lamont. Some gang initiation thing. He took my cash, all thirty dollars of it, slammed me across the face with his pistol and ran away. I never saw him again. I went to his house but his mother wouldn't talk to me, so I gave up. A couple of years later he was killed in a gang fight."

Caroline closed her eyes and felt tears leak onto her cheeks. No wonder he was so pessimistic about the kids.

Ford shook his head. "Don't cry. It was a lesson I had to learn. About what works. What doesn't."

She slid off the rock and took a step toward him. Then

she glanced over at the creek and stayed where she was. "That's a terrible experience to have gone through. I'm not surprised you're wary."

"But?"

"But being disappointed with one person—even failing to save them—doesn't excuse us from attempting to help someone else. We have to keep trying. Otherwise, the world declines into chaos."

Ford shook his head, smiling. "I hate to break it to you, but the world is already in chaos."

"So we ought to be working to straighten things out. With enough people helping, it can be done."

"What can be done?" Without their noticing, Dylan had joined them.

"Saving the world," Ford explained.

Caroline nodded. "As much of it as you can reach, anyway."

Dylan glanced from one of them to the other. "That's Garrett's job."

She couldn't help but laugh and was glad to see Ford grin. "Maybe we should leave it to him."

"Definitely. He's got the right connections. For now, though, he's pulled out the ice-cream maker and is expecting extra arms to help crank it. I figured there were a few down here."

"What a terrific idea! Let's get the kids back to the house." She started to follow Dylan toward the creek but stopped and faced Ford. "You're great with them, you know. You *are* making a difference."

She didn't wait for an answer, and as she watched him keep himself apart for the rest of the evening, she decided he hadn't been convinced.

WEDNESDAY MORNING, TENSION ran high as the kids got ready for their first riding lesson. Thomas camouflaged his own nerves by mocking someone else's—Lizzie, in particular—and Caroline had to reprimand him several times. The small size of the pony reassured Lizzie, however, and she climbed onto Major's back with only a little hesitation.

"He's a nice pony," Lizzie said, with pride in her voice. "I'm glad he likes me."

Caroline smiled at her. "Having a horse trust you is one of the best feelings in the world. We have to be careful to honor that trust. Now, just sit here while we get everybody else ready to ride."

She brought Becky into the corral next and helped her saddle the Appaloosa. "Do you want to use the mounting block? Or do you want to pull up from the ground?"

Becky nodded in determination. "I want to get on from the ground." With a little boost from Caroline, she did drag herself all the way into the saddle.

By the time Lena got settled, Nate, Thomas and Justino had mounted. Only Marcos remained standing.

Ford stood beside him. "Want a leg up?"

"Nah, man. I got this." Having watched the girls get on from the ground, Marcos could do no less. "Just hold the stupid horse." He started to lift his left foot to the stirrup.

But Ford clamped a hand on his shoulder and turned him around so fast the boy fell back against the horse's side. "No one," he said in a stern voice, "rides an animal on this property with that kind of attitude."

Marcos stared at him, eyes wide. "What is your problem?"

Garrett came up, pulled the reins from Ford's hand and moved the horse away. Hands on his hips, Ford took a step closer to Marcos, glaring down at him. "My problem is you. Either change your attitude and have some respect for the people and animals on this ranch, or go pack your stuff. You've got one minute to make your choice." He raised a hand and kept his eyes on his watch.

"No problem. I'm outta here." Marcos stomped toward the gate.

No one tried to stop him.

But when he got to the gate, he clutched the metal bars and stood without moving. Without opening the panel to leave.

"Time," Ford called.

Another few seconds went by. Caroline held her breath.

Slowly, Marcos turned. He walked across the corral to stand in front of Ford. His shoulders lifted and fell as he stared at the dirt between their booted feet. "Sorry," he said. "I'll...do better." He lifted his head. "Can I ride now?"

Ford held the boy's gaze for a long moment. Finally, he nodded toward Garrett. "Get on."

Caroline heard everybody in the corral give a sigh of relief.

With Marcos in the saddle, Dylan brought Sundance, saddled and bridled, over to Ford. The cowboy lawyer showed them all how it was done, stepping his foot into the stirrup and swinging his leg in a fluid arc across the horse to sit down lightly. Caroline made a sound of pure admiration at the sight.

"We're going to walk around the corral," he told the kids. "I'm the leader. I'll be in front of Lizzie and Major. Your horse will probably just follow the one in front of you. If he or she is a little slow getting started, kick with both legs. Caroline, Garrett and Dylan are here in case anybody has trouble." He checked out each kid individually and then nodded. "Let's ride."

Without prompting, Major followed Sundance. The rest of the horses fell quietly into line and, in less than a minute, all of them were riding.

If Caroline had known a week ago that she would have tears in her eyes because a group of kids was walking horses in a small, enclosed circle, she would have laughed. She was laughing now, despite the tears. They were all working so hard, just sitting there!

Ford led them in a right-hand circle for five or six circuits. He crossed the corral and changed directions, causing a wobble or two among the kids but none among the horses—they stayed quiet and calm. Eventually he led them in figure eights, straight lines across the middle and even a serpentine pattern. Nobody complained, and some of the kids—Becky, Lena, Nate and even Marcos—started to relax and enjoy themselves.

With one last circle to the left, Ford brought them to a halt at about the same place they'd started on the corral fence. He shifted Sundance around to face them. "Great job, all of you. You stayed on, you kept in line—that's real progress from the first afternoon."

There were grins from every direction, a couple of cautious fist pumps.

"We're going to get off for a while." That announcement was greeted with protests. "Have some lunch? We'll go for another ride this afternoon. The horses will stay saddled, but we'll loosen the girth to give them room and put the halter on so they can eat some hay and drink. Stay in the saddle and we'll come around to help you get off."

The dismounting process wasn't as long as getting everybody on, but more than one stomach growled before everybody's feet hit the dirt. Each kid went into the barn to get a flake of hay for their horse, hang up the bridle, put up the grooming bucket. They all walked a little stiffly to the gate, and the last one through—Nate—double-checked to be sure it was latched.

Then the excited chatter broke out. "It's a long way down!"

"I got him to turn with just a little pull…"

"She stopped right away when I asked…"

"Nobody fell off!"

Caroline stood with Garrett and Dylan, watching with a grin as the group moved away, comparing exploits and sharing their pride in what they'd just accomplished.

"Well, I'm exhausted." Dylan took off his hat and rubbed a hand over his hair. "And all I did was stand here."

"Watching was the hard part." Garrett started toward the barn. "I'm grabbing a soda while they fool around for a few minutes. Want one, Caroline?"

"Sure." She went into the barn, expecting to meet up with Ford. But by the time she'd reached the front door, she had to accept the fact that he wasn't there.

Dylan had come to the same conclusion. "Where's Ford? Has he pulled another disappearing act, like last night at dinner?"

"Maybe he went to check on Wyatt," Garrett suggested. At that moment Wyatt walked out onto the porch of the ranch house, and Ford wasn't with him. "Or maybe not."

"Come to think of it…" Dylan headed into the barn. He rejoined them in less than a minute. "Sundance isn't in the corral. Ford's out riding. Or doing something on horseback. Actually working, maybe. We haven't done much of that this week."

Garrett chuckled. "A few days off won't cause a big problem. Maybe he's avoiding the kids' attempts at cooking."

But Caroline thought Ford might just be avoiding her.

By DINNERTIME ON FRIDAY, Nate felt like a seasoned ranch hand. And he loved it. He got up earlier in the morning than he ever had during the school year, but knowing he'd be riding Lady Blue made it okay.

Not just riding in circles around the corral, either. Mr. Ford had taken them out into the big pasture where the

horses grazed and, as he put it, "turned you kids loose."
Each rider was free to go wherever they wanted. On
Thursday, going down a little hill, Blue broke into a jog.
Instead of being scared, Nate just went with her, sens-
ing her body shift underneath him and trying to match
his movements with hers. The wind brushed his face as
they went faster, and he decided right then that he would
spend the rest of his life with horses. He wasn't sure how
or where, yet, but he would do whatever it took to experience this kind of freedom as part of every single day.

When he wasn't in the saddle, he spent his days in the
kitchen, cooking or cleaning up, usually both. Every so
often, Marcos would give him a look, just to remind him
the deal still held. Because the grown-ups took turns supervising, nobody picked up on the fact that he was always
there. The other kids noticed, of course, but they had no
reason to say anything and plenty of reason not to, since
Marcos pretty much told them what to do and when to do
it. He was big enough and cocky enough to get his way,
or to make somebody wish he had.

Dinner tonight was no different. Nate helped Lizzie
and Lena put together a noodle and hamburger casserole,
plus a salad and garlic bread. Once dinner was finished,
he started taking the dishes off the table.

"You wash." Thomas elbowed him in the side. "Marcos says so."

Marcos always said so. Nate didn't bother answering.

Miss Caroline came into the kitchen—she always stayed
around when Thomas and Justino did cleanup, to be sure
everything got done. Nate kept his head down as he ran
water in the sink, hoping not to attract attention.

But tonight she noticed. "Nate, you cooked with Lizzie
and Lena, didn't you? You don't have to clean up, too.
Somebody else can wash the dishes."

"I don't mind." He could see disaster coming, like he

was standing on the railroad tracks with a freight train headed directly at him.

"There are plenty of people to share the work. Thomas, you can take over the dishes. Justino can dry. Becky's wiping the table…" She surveyed the four of them and frowned. "Where's Marcos?"

Nobody said anything.

"He's part of your group, right?"

Still no answer.

Miss Caroline stood for a minute with her hands on her hips. "This isn't the first meal when Nate has worked for Marcos, is it? Becky?"

Becky shook her head.

"Nate, come with me."

He followed her outside. Lizzie and Lena were on the porch of the cabin with their phones. Marcos was nowhere in sight.

"What's going on?" She put a hand on his shoulder and made him face her. "Why are you doing Marcos's work?"

"He wanted me to."

"But you didn't have to agree. Why would you do that?"

Nate shrugged. "He's bigger than me."

"Did he threaten you?"

"N-no." He couldn't lie, even if it got him into more trouble.

She stared at him, frowning. "This has to stop. I'm going to find Marcos and get the story from him. No matter what, you don't do his work again. It's not good for him. Understand?"

"I guess so."

"Okay. Go hang out for a while. Tonight's TV night, if you're interested."

"Sure." He went back in and switched on the set, but he sat there without watching.

What would Marcos say? If Miss Caroline found out

that Nate had left the ranch, would she be mad enough to send him home?

Had he ridden Lady Blue for the last time?

CAROLINE FOUND MARCOS in the last place she expected— talking to Ford.

They were standing in the corral, leaning on the fence for the horses' pasture and watching the sun sink below the mountains. They seemed to have established a rapport, and she almost hated to disturb them.

Then she remembered Nate, who'd been working in the kitchen all week while Marcos escaped any responsibility. "Marcos?" She projected her voice with all the force she could muster. "Marcos!"

The two males jerked around. They watched her approach them across the corral, staying where they were.

She stopped directly in front of Marcos, breathing hard, though more from the anger possessing her than the effort of striding across the dirt. "You're cheating."

"I don't know what you're talking about." But guilt kept his gaze away from hers.

"You forced Nate to take your kitchen duty. Practically all week long, he's been doing your job."

Ford stiffened. "Is that right?"

Marcos shrugged. "How would I make him? I didn't beat him up or nothing."

"You're a big guy, which is what counts. Well, your holiday is over. You're going home."

She wasn't prepared for the way his face changed. In a moment, he went from an arrogant, combative teenager to a chastened and worried boy.

"I don't want to leave."

"You've been nothing but trouble all week, Marcos. How am I supposed to accept that you want to stay?"

"I'll do better. I'll do my jobs."

"He probably means it," Ford said. "Right now."

Caroline kept her eyes on Marcos. "Why should I believe you?"

The boy shook his head. "No reason. I have to prove it."

Now she glanced at Ford, trying to read his reaction. Marcos could be manipulating her, pretending a penitence he was far from feeling because he figured she'd give in.

Ford's doubt showed in the thin line of his mouth, the frown in his eyes. He would probably advise against trusting Marcos again, as his experience with Lamont still weighed heavily on him.

But Caroline had to believe in the best of human nature. She'd staked her life—lost her family—for the chance to make a difference with kids just like Marcos. Surrender was not an option.

"I'll give you one last chance," she said, ignoring Ford's exasperated breath. "But no more, Marcos. If you cause problems again, throw another tantrum, refuse to cooperate—I won't discuss it or debate it. You will go home."

"Right. I got it. Can I go now?"

"Yes."

He crossed to the barn at a near run and disappeared inside. Exhausted from just the last few minutes, Caroline let her shoulders slump. She put a hand to her temple, where a headache had started to throb.

"That," Ford said quietly, "was a big mistake."

CAROLINE STRAIGHTENED HER spine and lifted her head. "I'm sure you think so," she said. "But I have to try."

"And I admire your hopefulness. I just hate for you to be disappointed."

"It's happened before." She began walking toward the barn.

Ford came up beside her. "You're talking about your dad?"

"Among many others I've tried to help over the years. People aren't perfect, Ford. They're going to make mistakes. You forgive them and go on."

"You make it sound easy."

Caroline stopped at the door to the barn and faced him. "You make it especially difficult." Dark had fallen, but he could discern her face by the light of a rising moon. "You're so worried about having all the bases covered, the risks managed, that you can't relax and just enjoy life. You never consider what you want, Ford. You only focus on what's safe."

"Not true." He set his hands against the wall on either side of her. "Lately, I'm thinking all the time about what I want. Like this—" Bending his head, he kissed her temple, her cheek, her ear. "And this." He trailed his fingers along her throat, let them rest at the pulse point above her breastbone. "This." He slipped his arm around her waist, pulled her against him and dove in to take her mouth. "I want you every minute of every day. Whether it's safe or not."

Caroline yielded, her arms around his neck drawing him even closer, her mouth opening underneath his. Ford groaned and released the reins on his desire, his body fully alive to the pleasure of her softness against him. He ran his hands over her slim back and then lower, shaping her bottom with his palms, pressing her even harder against him. Her shirttail came loose, and now his hands were on her skin, so smooth and warm. Kisses seared between them, lips and tongues searching, always searching for more. At the brink of sanity, Ford wrapped an arm around her waist and the other under her bottom and lifted Caroline off the ground, with her shoulders against the wall. She wrapped her legs around his hips.

The night filled with fire.

He wasn't sure what returned him to consciousness. Maybe some wisp of a gentleman's code floating through his brain that said you didn't take a woman you cared about against the wall of a barn. Ford hoped so, anyway. All he knew was that he had to stop now. Or he wouldn't be able to stop at all.

"Shh, shh." He eased Caroline to the floor, allowed some air to flow between his body and hers. She kept kissing him, and he couldn't—wouldn't—make her stop, but he tried to lower the heat, slow the tempo, somehow wind down their desire to something he could control.

Eventually, she lowered her head and took in a ragged breath. Then she dropped her chin to rest her forehead against his chest. After a while she said, "Thanks."

He gave a ghost of a laugh. "Anytime."

"No, I mean for stopping."

"I can't say it was my pleasure."

"No. But smart."

"Yeah." He hesitated awhile, then decided he had to ask. "Caroline, what about Garrett?"

She didn't lift her head. "What about him?"

"Are you...together?"

Now she stared up at him, her forehead wrinkled. "No. Close friends, that's all." In the next moment she pulled away and walked a few steps off before turning to stare at him. "Why in the world do you ask? Do you honestly believe I would—would act this way with you if Garrett and I had a romantic relationship?"

"I didn't mean—"

"I don't go around making love with just any guy who happens to be hanging around."

"Caroline—"

"Maybe you expect it from the women you meet out there in almighty San Francisco, but I'm not that kind of person. I save my kisses for people I lo—care about, thank you very much." She stomped farther into the barn, toward the front door, tucking in her shirt as she went.

Ford didn't follow. He could predict what would happen if he caught up with her in the dark.

Instead, he crossed his arms against the wall and leaned his head into them. He needed a few more minutes to calm down. Caroline had nearly blown his fuse with her kisses. Those kisses she saved for the people she lo—

Love? What other word would she have meant? Had Caroline just confessed that she loved him? Was he ready to admit the same thing?

And what the hell was he supposed to do about it?

Chapter Ten

The teenagers tried to be cool, but their excitement over going to the rodeo was all too obvious. Even their Saturday cleaning chores didn't dim the air of expectation. By lunch, they could hardly sit still in their chairs. Thomas, Marcos, Justino and Becky finished kitchen cleanup in record time, with no prompting from Caroline. She'd announced that they'd be leaving the ranch at two o'clock, but by one thirty everyone had found a place on the house porch, as if afraid of getting left behind.

By luck or by design, Dylan and Garrett rode together in Wyatt's truck, leaving Ford as a passenger in the van with Caroline and the kids. Still nursing her hurt feelings, Caroline had managed to avoid him all day, and didn't plan to converse with him except in case of an emergency.

For a change, though, Ford didn't challenge her to communicate—he sat on his side of the van without speaking, staring straight ahead. After a few miles of absolute quiet, Caroline decided she would have to be the one to break the silence.

"So who has been to a rodeo before?" None of the kids answered. "Nobody?"

"When I was a little kid, my dad went to rodeos." Nate's quiet voice came from the rear of the van. "But that was years ago."

Becky spoke up. "You went, didn't you, Miss Caroline?"

"I spent a lot of time at rodeos. I would go with my dad when I was young, because he supplied horses and bulls for the events. I started barrel racing myself, and went to compete." She decided not to let Ford escape contributing. "Mr. Ford and his brothers went to the rodeo, too."

Thomas voiced his skepticism. "Bet you never rode in one, though."

Ford stirred in his seat. "Bet you'd lose. We competed all through high school. Miss Caroline isn't giving you the whole story, though. She rode for her college in barrel racing. She's a real champion."

"What kind of riding does a rodeo have, anyway?" Lizzie asked. "I've never watched one, even on TV."

"Bull riding," Thomas said. "Bareback horses."

"They're called bucking broncs." Marcos corrected him. "Also saddle broncs. Where the horse wears a saddle."

"Steer roping," Justino added. "But the bull riders are the best. You can get killed by those things."

"What event did you ride in, Mr. Ford?" That was Nate again.

Looking flushed, Ford cleared his throat. "I tried all the rough-stock events, as they're called—the bulls, the saddle broncs and bareback. But most often I rode the bulls."

The kids whistled and cheered. "Can you ride today?" For the first time all week, Justino showed some enthusiasm. "That would be cool to watch."

"I haven't ridden in years." Ford shook his head. "And you have to sign up in advance."

But when they reached the rodeo grounds and got out of the van, an announcement over the loudspeaker caught their attention. "There's still a chance to sign up, ladies and gents, for the rough-stock events and barrel racing!

We're accepting all competitors, so if you've got the itch to show off your rodeo skills this afternoon, here's your opportunity!"

The boys, even Nate, began pestering Ford. "You gotta do it," Marcos said.

"Come on, man." Thomas was almost jumping up and down. "We want to see you ride."

Ford looked at Caroline. "Above and beyond the call of duty, right?"

"Definitely. We don't want you getting hurt." But that, she realized immediately, was the wrong thing to say.

He stared at her, a steely glint in his eyes. "You don't trust me to stay on?"

Fear drilled into her chest. "You said yourself, it's been years since you rode."

"Some things you don't forget. For instance, *you* could ride in the barrel races."

Aware of the kids circled around them, listening, she didn't inform him he was crazy. "I don't have a horse."

"That might not be a problem. Come on, kids."

In the next moment, Ford and the teenagers headed over to the rodeo office. With a helpless glance at the other Marshall brothers, Caroline followed.

She arrived to hear the rodeo secretary assuring Ford that they did have horses available for barrel racers without one. "Can't guarantee their speed, but we got a few extras, courtesy of the Donnelly Ranch outfit. They supplied all the stock for today's show."

Great. Her dad's horses—chances were she had ridden one or two of them. And did that mean she'd be running into him while trying to keep control of this bunch of teenagers? Would he say something she'd regret?

"Come on, Miss Caroline." Lena tugged on her shirt-sleeve. "You've gotta show us how you ride."

"The boys have a bull rider," Lizzie added. "We ought to have a barrel racer on our side."

Becky's excited face echoed her friend's opinion.

And so, against her better judgment, Caroline entered the barrel racing event. Garrett was shaking his head as she and Ford steered the kids toward them.

"You two are crazy," he said. "You're both ten years or more—" he cocked an eyebrow at Ford "—out of practice."

"The bull won't realize that." Ford held up his entry sheet. "Oh, great—his name is Nutcracker."

Caroline folded her lips on a smile, but his brothers howled in laughter. Thomas, Marcos and Justino got the joke and snickered. The girls and Nate looked puzzled.

"I'll explain it to you later," Justino told Lena. "Then you can explain it to them." He nodded at Becky and Lizzie.

Once inside the rodeo gates, all the kids immediately wanted food. And each of them wanted something different, which made supervising impossible. Caroline distributed cash and a warning to meet her at the corner of the bleachers in fifteen minutes so they could all get seated.

"They're finishing up the team roping," Dylan reported. "We missed the bareback riding."

"Probably just as well," Ford said. "The kids would want to be out in the field trying to ride without saddles." He glanced over at Wyatt. "Maybe you should go and find a seat. We'll probably be a while."

"No, I like standing here just fine." Wyatt adjusted the set of his hat and gazed out over the crowd. "I'm thinking you're the one who'll be having trouble standing once you get on that bull. You're insane, letting these kids goad you into it."

"Probably." Ford sounded a little annoyed himself. "If

I get into trouble, I'll bail out. I do remember how to fall off."

Dylan leaned over to speak into Caroline's ear. "That's them having an argument."

She nodded. "I can tell."

Though it took more than fifteen minutes, all the kids showed up at the appointed place, various types of food in their hands and expectation on their faces. Caroline sent Thomas and Marcos in first. "Find a place where all of us can sit together."

And they did—on the highest row, of course. If the climb bothered Wyatt, he didn't let on. And if seeing Wyatt climb to the top of the bleachers bothered Ford, the only clue was the straight line of his mouth, the hard set of his jaw. He didn't say a word.

There were eight riders in the saddle bronc event, and Caroline could only grin as the teenagers around her got into the rodeo spirit. They sat forward as horse and rider erupted from the chute, gasping at turns and kicks and spins, cheering as the cowboy stayed on for a full eight seconds and moaning in sympathy for the ones who didn't make it that long. They talked over each competitor's performance, consulting the Marshall brothers on the fine details. Caroline was happy that all of them—brothers and kids alike—were having a fun.

When the steer wrestling started, she stood up and got everybody's attention. "I'm going down to meet my horse and get ready to race. Any questions before I go?"

With the shaking of a few heads, the kids quickly refocused on the action in the arena.

Caroline chuckled and started to make her way down the bleachers.

In the next moment, she realized Ford was coming down behind her.

She turned to confront him, which meant gazing a long way up. "What are you doing?"

"I planned to walk you over to the pens."

"You don't have to do that."

"Do you mind?" His gaze was more intense than the simple question called for.

"N-no. Of course not." She tried to dispel the tension. "No respectable cowgirl would mind walking through the rodeo grounds with a handsome cowboy at her side."

"Thanks for the tip." He waved her on, leaving her no option but to continue down the steps and out of the arena, with Ford right behind her.

Walking past the food trucks and the booths selling T-shirts, fancy belt buckles and cheap jewelry, Caroline searched for something to say. "I bet you haven't been to a rodeo—even to watch—since you went to college."

"Have you? Since you left the team?"

"I go with friends occasionally. It's a fun way to spend a Saturday night."

"Especially if you're not the one getting bucked off."

"That's probably true." She stopped and put a hand on his arm. "You really don't have to make this ride. The kids will cope if you withdraw."

His warm fingers covered hers. "Don't worry. I'll be okay."

"I would feel awful if you got hurt." She'd forgotten she was trying to be mad at him.

"How will you feel when I come off just fine?" The question seemed more important than the words would suggest.

"I—I—"

The loudspeaker crackled. "All barrel racing competitors should report to check-in for their event. Ladies, we're waiting for you!"

Ford tilted his head. "Better get going."

They jogged toward the horse pens and arrived at the sign-up table just as the last person in line finished. "I'm Caroline Donnelly," she said, panting a little. "I'll need a horse."

"Sure thing," the woman at the table said, checking her list. "It's funny that you're a Donnelly, too. These horses come from the Donnelly Quarter Horse Ranch."

"Yes. Funny." She grimaced at Ford and got a commiserating frown in return.

"So our extras are in that pen right over there. They're for sale, too, in case you're interested. Pick whichever one you want, and have a great ride."

Caroline glanced at the horses inside the fence and gasped. "He didn't!"

Ford followed her to the pen. "You recognize these horses?"

"I know the palomino. I raised her from a foal. She was my horse when I lived at ho—when I still lived at the ranch. Her name is Medallion. I called her Allie." She slipped through the gate, and Ford latched it behind her. "Allie? Remember me, Allie girl?"

The golden horse lifted her head at the sound of Caroline's voice. Then she whickered in greeting.

"Hey, lady, how are you?" Caroline ran her hand along the mare's neck, noticing the dirt in her coat, the untrimmed length of her mane. "Somebody's not brushing you, are they?" She kept her voice soft and friendly, despite her distress. "You need a beauty treatment, hmm?" Allie rubbed her forehead against Caroline's sleeve, leaving behind some dry, dusty hair.

Ford had come around on the outside to where Caroline stood with the horse. "Looks like she's been turned out for quite a while. Will she be okay to ride?"

"I trust her. Will you tell the secretary which horse I've chosen?"

"Sure thing."

Caroline untied Allie's rope from the fence and led her out of the pen. "Did you come with a bridle, girl? You got one of the old, beat-up saddles, didn't you?" But it still had a brass plaque tacked on saying, "Donnelly Ranch."

Ford came over holding a bridle. "The secretary gave me this for you."

"Great." Caroline slipped the bridle into place, noting that it hadn't been oiled or even cleaned recently. "Secondhand gear, Allie. But we're gonna have a nice fast run, aren't we? Do our best out there with those barrels?"

She looked at Ford. "Guess we're set."

He grinned. "Leg up?"

"Sure." With her left foot in the stirrup she bent her knee and felt Ford take hold. In one easy move she swung into the saddle. Settling, she said, "We work well together."

"I noticed that." He stood beside her, with a hand on her calf. "I'm going to go out front so I can watch. Have fun."

"Thanks." She and Allie took their places as last in line, waiting as the nine horses ahead of them took a run at the barrel pattern out in the arena. Finally, it was their turn. They moved into the alley and started at a lope, getting faster and faster, till they burst out onto open ground.

"Go, Allie," Caroline shouted, kicking her heels. "Go!"

FORD FOUND AN empty spot on the arena wall and stepped into it, propping his folded arms on top. One by one the barrel racers shot out, following the cloverleaf pattern of the race. Most of the riders were local, and the times were on the slow side—eighteen, twenty seconds or more. Caroline had a decent chance of actually winning the event.

He tensed up as rider nine completed her pattern and crossed the finish line. In a couple of seconds, *whoosh*, Caroline and Allie dashed into sight, running for the left-hand barrel. A quick loop around and they were crossing to his right. From appearances, Caroline might have been practicing every day of the past ten years, while Allie was a natural for the sport. From the second barrel they flew to the third, and were halfway around when, somehow, they knocked into the barrel. As the big drum teetered, Caroline and Allie headed for the finish. Just before they crossed the line, the barrel fell.

She'd done a great run—fourteen and a half seconds. But the upended barrel would add five seconds to her time.

The announcer commiserated. "Too bad for our last contender, Caroline Donnelly. But her time still puts her in third place for the event. Our barrel race concludes with Cindy Fremont in first with eighteen point one five seconds, Gail Valdes with nineteen point three two seconds and Caroline Donnelly in third with nineteen point five six seconds. Congratulations, ladies! Bull riding is up next, folks, so get ready for more rodeo excitement!"

"Oh, yeah." Ford rolled his eyes. He realized this was one of the dumber stunts he'd pulled since actually becoming an adult. He wasn't nearly as sure he'd come out of it okay as he'd pretended to be with Caroline. If his brothers suspected the truth, they'd kept their mouths shut.

Thing was, the kids had a stake in watching him ride. They'd been taking risks because he'd been telling them to—working with and getting on their horses, walking and jogging in the field, getting off again. In their view, they'd simply challenged him to take the same kind of risk. Ford figured he owed them that much after making demands on them all week long.

Withdrawing would cost him all the authority he'd earned with them, making this next week even harder than the first. The teenagers wouldn't trust him anymore. Wouldn't respect him. Too many people in their lives offered only disappointment. One of the major aims of Caroline's project was to provide these kids with role models they could count on.

And so he would ride. He borrowed a glove and spurs from a guy he knew who happened to be working at the rodeo, and rented a rope rigging from one of the other competitors. Six bulls would take a shot at dumping six cowboys.

Until, finally, Nutcracker and he would get to do their own crazy dance.

NATE REMEMBERED RODEOS as places where his dad hung out with a bunch of loud, laughing men, almost never won money, got mad drunk and yelled at his mom to "keep the kid quiet, for God's sake."

Today was totally different and Nate had soaked up every minute. He'd enjoyed the cattle, the horses—so many horses!—the riders and ropers and the kids riding baby cows. Thomas, Marcos and Justino had spent the afternoon bragging about what they would do if they could compete, but Nate didn't want to enter an event, wasn't into speed or power or crazy stunts like Mr. Ford's bull riding. He just enjoyed watching.

Miss Caroline came up the bleacher steps fluttering her yellow ribbon above her head. "Not bad for an old lady, huh?" she asked, sitting down between Lizzie and Lena. "That was so much fun! I'd forgotten how great it feels to ride so fast."

"You were awesome," Becky gushed. "Even without fancy chaps and stuff, you rode better than all the other girls."

"I want to do that," Lizzie said. Everybody else stared at her in surprise. "I want to barrel race."

"We can work on that at the ranch," Miss Caroline said, glancing behind her to Mr. Dylan and Mr. Garrett. "We'll set up some barrels and run some patterns. You and Major will be a good pair."

"Is that all girls are allowed to do?" Lena pouted. "Why aren't there other rodeo events for us?"

"The Women's Pro Rodeo Association sponsors shows where women ride bulls and broncs as well as compete in barrel racing," Miss Caroline said.

"That's what I want to do." Lena crossed her arms and nodded. "I want to ride broncs." Thomas and Marcos laughed at the idea. "Shut up, you two. I can if I want to."

"Ladies and gents," the announcer said over the loud-speaker, "we've arrived at the final event of the day—bull riding. We've got seven contenders ready to pit their strength against these fine animals, courtesy of the Don-nelly Ranch, so let's get started. First up, number 401, Travis Bradley."

Nate's blood froze. His heart stopped beating. Why would his dad be here? He hadn't ridden in a rodeo since Amber was born. Why now? What did it mean?

The gate swung open, and the big bull hopped out, bucking like he meant to kick out the sky. Nate's dad seemed pretty small up on top, with one hand above his head and one hand holding the rope to stay on.

But he came off quickly. As the bull spun around on his front legs, still kicking his hind ones, Travis Bradley flew into the air and landed facedown in the dirt. The buzzer sounded as he scrambled to his feet and ran for the fence, just inches in front of the horns coming after him.

Another failure. Another excuse to drink. A reason to be mad and hit people who couldn't defend themselves.

Nate turned to Mr. Garrett, who was sitting next to him. "I have to go down there."

"To the pens? Why?"

"I—I need to see if my mom's there. If she's okay."

Mr. Garrett narrowed his eyes. "Wait. Travis Bradley is your dad?"

Nate nodded. "He gets mad when he loses."

"I'll go with you."

"No!" Nate put out a hand. "It will be worse if somebody's there. Just let me go find my mom. I promise I'll come back. Please?"

"Go ahead. I'll explain to Caroline."

Even though he ran, it seemed to take forever to get through the crowd and find his way behind the bull pens. Cowboys sat on the fences and stood around talking, but he didn't see the blue-checked shirt his dad was wearing. So many corners and dead ends to search—he kept looking, kept listening, and Nate didn't know whether finding him would be a good thing or bad.

As he came around one corner, he ran into a cowboy. "Sorry, mister," Nate said, peering beyond him. "I'm sorry."

"Whoa, there." The man clapped a hand on his shoulder. "What are you doing here, Nate?"

He glanced up and recognized Mr. Ford. "Oh. I'm looking for my...for my dad. He just rode."

"I saw him head toward the trailers. Come on."

"That's okay. You have to ride. I can find him."

There was no arguing with the hand on his shoulder. "I've got a couple of minutes."

But they didn't have to go far—his dad had barely reached the exit before losing his temper.

"Damn clown let that bull just about gore me." He took a swig from the bottle he was holding. "That's the way it is with these stupid little shows—can't get a decent crew to help a rider out. I coulda been killed."

Nate's mom was there, holding Amber on her hip, and she saw him coming. Her eyes widened, and she shook her head, warning him off.

But his dad noticed the motion, and wheeled around. "What the hell are you doing here? Thought you was playing cowboy at some ranch near town." He frowned as he eyed Mr. Ford. "Who are you and what are you doin' with my son?"

"I'm Ford Marshall. Nate's been staying at my brother's ranch this week. He came down to make sure you're okay after that fall."

"No thanks to any of the crew out there." He took another drink. "What's your problem, boy? You look downright puny. Ain't they feedin' you at this fancy ranch you're on?"

"No. I mean, sure, I get plenty to eat." He never could talk to his dad. It didn't matter what he said, it was always wrong. "Is everything all right?" Nate glanced at his mom, trying to ask more with his face than with his words.

"We're fine, son. Just fine." She was wearing sunglasses, but Nate didn't think he imagined another bruise high on her cheek. There was definitely one on her wrist. "Go on back to your friends, now. We're getting ready to head home." The tilt of her head made it a plea. "Go on."

He turned and left them there, her and Amber, though it just about killed him.

But he'd decided what he was going to do.

AFTER MEETING UP with Nate's dad, riding Nutcracker seemed anticlimactic. Ford climbed into the pen, sat down and set his legs and then wound the rope tightly around his palm. With his free hand, he jammed his hat down on his head. He hoped it didn't get too dirty—it was one of his best ones.

The guy on the gate glanced over. "Ready, cowboy?"

Ford set his teeth and nodded.

The gate clanged, and they were out in the arena, with Nutcracker doing his best to live up to the name. For-

ward, back, left, right—the bull jerked him around like
a rag doll.

Breathe, Ford thought. *Stick it*. And then the craziest
notion of all in this particular situation. *Caroline*.

He didn't remember exactly when or how he got off—
he found himself scrambling across the dirt as the rodeo
clowns distracted Nutcracker from an understandable desire to kill the pesky human who'd dared to ride him.
Breathing hard, Ford retrieved his filthy hat, climbed behind the arena wall and stood searching the crowd as he
waited for his score. Where were they? He couldn't find
any of the kids, or Wyatt, or...

The announcement streamed out loud and clear.
"That'll be a terrific score of 75 for Ford Marshall and
Nutcracker. Let's give a big hand, folks, for our bull rid-
ing winner tonight, Mr. Ford Marshall!"

Suddenly, he was surrounded—Thomas and Marcos,
Justino and Lena, Lizzie and Becky and Nate, patting him
on the shoulder and grinning, punching him in the arm,
grabbing both his hands. He was getting more beat up by
the kids than he had been by the bull.

His brothers stood a few feet off, smiling and shaking
their heads. And there was Caroline, eyes shining, hands
gripped together as she mouthed, "You are so crazy."

He grinned at her. *Yeah, maybe*. But occasionally being
crazy paid off. And this might be one of those times. Evidently taking a risk could produce success, after all.

They headed toward the big tent for dinner—a Western barbecue put on by local civic associations. The kids
lagged behind, investigating the souvenir booths. Wyatt
had stopped to talk to a rancher he knew, and he was
joined by Garrett and Dylan.

"I guess we'd better wait for them," Caroline said, turning around to look back at the stragglers. "I want to keep
everybody together."

Ford, facing forward, noticed a tall man in a Western-cut jacket striding toward them with the finesse of a bulldozer. He pivoted, intending to warn her. "Caroline."

"I wish they'd hurry, though," she continued. "I'm hungry enough to eat one of those bulls whole."

"Caroline." He put a hand on her shoulder, and she looked at him in question. "Your dad—"

His warning came too late. In the next moment, George Donnelly started to brush past them.

Caroline caught him by the coat sleeve. "Daddy?"

George Donnelly whipped his head around. "What are you doing here?" For an instant, Ford thought he saw surprise and, maybe, gladness flash in Donnelly's gaze.

Then his dark eyes moved to Ford's face. "Who's this?"

"Ford Marshall." He didn't move to shake the man's hand.

Donnelly nodded. "One of *them*." His gaze flicked to Caroline again. "What do you want?"

"To say hello?" She glanced at the crowd. "Is Mom here? Reid?"

He frowned. "The whereabouts of my family are not your concern."

At the brusque answer, Caroline staggered, as if the ground had shifted under her. She let her hand fall to her side.

Her father didn't care. "I have to go." He turned…and came face-to-face with seven teenagers, plus the three Marshall brothers standing behind them. "What is this? Am I being mugged?"

"That's enough, Mr. Donnelly." Ford stepped up beside him. "You can be polite."

"I can be done with this." He moved forward, but the kids didn't yield. "You want to spend your life with juvenile delinquents and small-time dirt farmers?" Shaking his head, he sent Caroline a look of pity. "You deserve what you get."

Shoulder first, he ploughed his way through the group. Dylan and Garrett separated to let him pass. "Good riddance," Wyatt told Donnelly's retreating figure, making no effort to be quiet.

Ford took Caroline's cold hand. "How about some food? Maybe not a whole bull, but we'll make the attempt." Other than knocking George Donnelly to the ground, he wasn't sure what else he could do to make this better for her.

Her green gaze stayed blank for a long moment. Then she shook her head and smiled…sort of. "Sure. Let's eat."

WHILE THEY STOOD in line to get their food, Ford leaned down to speak softly in Caroline's ear. "Are you okay?"

She shrugged one shoulder. "I shouldn't have expected anything different. I should have just let him go by." There had been a moment, as her dad walked away, when she'd almost broken down. Losing him again had seared like having an arm cut off.

Luckily, Ford had distracted her. The warmth of his hand over hers had reminded her that there were people she cared about and who cared about her. The teenagers made a point of entertaining her during the meal with stories and jokes, not mentioning the encounter with her dad even once. Their sensitivity surprised her. A couple of times she had to blink away grateful tears.

Of course, the tiny hope she'd nourished that her father might someday relent had just died, painfully and in public. She would have to go on without him and without her brother, who'd taken his side. Staying in touch with her mom would be the best she could do.

But now she knew she wasn't alone in the world. She'd grown close to the Marshalls—Wyatt and Garrett and Dylan were almost like brothers. Working with the kids this week had created another circle of special relationships. She had a connection with each of them. They were all her family, in the very best sense of the word.

Ford was in a class by himself, in every possible way. What would happen between them, though, Caroline couldn't begin to guess.

As the sun began to set, the sound of live music filtered through the crowd's noise. People began to drift toward the big metal building beside the arena, where a barn dance would be held.

"Can we go to the dance?" Lena clapped her hands. "Please, can we go?"

Caroline focused on the kids gathered in front of her. "There are rules," she said firmly. "You stay inside the building. No wandering out into the dark. Even if you meet somebody you know, do not go outside with them. And inside, you stay with one of our group—don't go to the bathroom or anywhere else by yourself. Is that clear?"

"Crystal," Thomas said. "Can we go now?"

She nodded, and they set off for the barn at a pace slightly slower than a run.

"Do you trust them to stick around?" Wyatt took an easier pace, which the other adults accommodated. "How can you be sure they won't take off? This is a pretty big crowd," he said as they reached the doorway. "Will we ever find them again?"

"They heard the rules," Ford said. "They should understand by now that they'll only get privileges if they obey those rules. I think they'll come back when we ask them to."

Caroline stopped in her tracks, staring at him in amazement.

Ford met her gaze. "What's wrong?"

"Did you hit your head on that ride? You don't sound like yourself at all."

"Maybe I learned a thing or two over the week, too."

"Really?"

Before he could answer, Dylan sauntered over. "Miss Caroline, would you care for a dance?"

Ford stepped between them. "Sorry, brother. She's already given the first dance to me." When Dylan opened his mouth to argue, Ford put his arm around her waist and walked her out onto the floor. In the next moment, they were doing a two-step.

She leaned back to look up at him. "I did?"

"You did." He sent her out to arm's length for a spin and pulled her in again, closer this time. "You don't want to dance with Dylan. Or Garrett. Or Wyatt," he murmured into her ear.

Caroline didn't protest the lack of space between their bodies. "What makes you so sure?"

"The way you kiss *me*."

She couldn't say anything for a long moment. "You're full of surprises tonight."

"I guess I needed some shaking up. Nutcracker did me a favor."

"I was scared to death for you."

"That makes two of us."

She laughed. "I don't believe you."

"I'm scared now, too."

Again she drew back to stare up at him. "Why?"

Ford held her gaze. "I've never been in love before."

Her pulse jumped, and she got a little dizzy. "Why are you confessing this in the midst of all these people?"

"You said we couldn't leave the building. The only other option for a little privacy was dancing." The music stopped and then started up again for a line dance. Keeping Caroline's hand, Ford located his brothers standing against a wall. He headed in the opposite direction.

Luckily, they found an empty corner where they could

have a little bit of privacy. Ford stood with his back to the crowd. "Just warn me if you see anybody coming."

"I will." She reached up and touched his jaw briefly. "But you can't kiss me here."

"I can think about it. You can think about it. That's almost good enough."

They stared at each other for a minute, while the air around them got warmer…hotter…stifling. The tension between them tightened unbearably.

Finally, Caroline made herself look away.

Ford shifted his weight and cleared his throat. "Okay, maybe not something we should think too hard about in public."

She covered her flushed face with shaking hands. "Probably not."

"Guess we'll have to stick to dancing. But later, maybe we could do a little guard duty. Make sure the kids stay where they belong. What do you say, Miss Caroline?"

"Sounds like a good precaution, Mr. Ford. We wouldn't want anybody roaming around loose in the dark."

"No, indeed." The music changed again, to a waltz. Before he could ask, Caroline grabbed his hand.

"In the meantime, cowboy," she said, smiling with all her heart, "come dance with me."

ALL THE KIDS fell asleep on the ride home. Ford drove the van and held Caroline's hand and didn't think beyond getting through the next hour until he could hold her in his arms.

His watch read almost 3:00 a.m. by the time he made his way to the house and to his room. He would have ignored his email until tomorrow, but he bumped the table while taking his boots off, which woke up the computer. His mail page came up on the screen.

A message from his assistant, entitled Urgent in red letters, caught his eye.

The office is in an uproar, she wrote. Lyle Cavendish marched into Price's office on Friday—without an appointment—to complain about the lack of progress on his case. Cavendish was Ford's most profitable client. Price smoothed things over, but once C left, he pitched a fit of his own and ordered a review of all your current files and an update on any résumés received in the last six months. There are interview calls going out next week. You'd better come back now if you're ever planning to.

Chapter Eleven

Monday morning Ford threw himself into the work with the kids and the ranch chores using every ounce of energy he possessed, all the while wondering how to fix the mess he'd made of his life.

The time frame for deciding between Wyoming and San Francisco had become hours instead of weeks or days. He could desert Caroline but maintain a secure future for his brothers and the Circle M Ranch. Or he could stay with the woman he loved and risk everything Henry MacPherson and the Marshalls had worked for all these years.

Or, he realized late in the afternoon, Caroline could come to San Francisco. He had assumed, at the beginning, that she wouldn't consider that option. But she was estranged from her family. And there were plenty of people who needed help on the West Coast. Perhaps all he had to do, to solve his dilemma, was ask.

He met her on the porch for "guard duty" Monday night. "Everybody in bed?" he asked, as he climbed the steps. "The boys seem to be settled."

"The girls are asleep. All this exercise has them so tired at night, they don't even stay up to play with their phones."

He sat down beside her on the double rocker and stretched his arm behind her shoulders. "There may be hope for them yet." When he bent his head, she met him halfway. "Mmm. I've been waiting for that all day."

"Me, too." Another kiss, this one lasting longer, going deeper. She tasted like the hot chocolate she'd whipped up earlier, while he was playing the guitar for the kids. When she drew away to take a deep breath, he kissed her temples, her eyes and the tip of her nose.

"What's this you're wrapped up in?" He tugged at the blanket she'd brought out from the house.

"It's cold out here."

"Funny, I'm feeling kind of heated."

"I'm getting warmer," she whispered.

Ford angled his body to bring them closer together. "Must be doing something right."

"Oh, yes." Desire blazed between them, her skin hot to his touch, his body burning for more contact, more connection…

"This is crazy," he said at last, exerting some control. "You're driving me crazy. And, God help me, I can't do anything about that here and now."

"I'm sorry." Caroline sat up straight and pulled her shirtfront together.

"No, don't be." He let his head drop back and took a deep breath. "But we deserve better than a front porch rocker, with one ear always listening for somebody coming along. So…" His hand closed over hers and held it tight. "So I'm asking you to come to California with me. To San Francisco."

Her eyes widened. "You mean—"

"As my wife, Caroline. I want to marry you."

Her lips parted, but she didn't say anything.

Ford shifted, facing her more directly. "Silence wasn't quite the reaction I was hoping for."

She pushed her hair behind her shoulders. "I'm not sure what to say."

"A simple 'yes' would work. I love you, Caroline. Maybe I always have. Maybe I was just waiting to find you again to start living my life. That's how it feels."

"I know," she said, after another pause. "I've felt that way, too. But—"

"They want me at the office." He might as well confess everything. "My job is at risk."

"I thought you would be here for the summer."

"Me, too. The senior partner has changed his mind about that. You don't have to come right away, though. I understand you have a commitment to the kids." He tried out a grin. "Besides, it takes a while to plan a wedding, right?"

She didn't return the smile. "How will Garrett and Dylan manage everything? The camp, the ranch work, Wyatt…"

Ford swallowed his impatience. "We might have to hire a couple of guys to deal with the cattle and chores." He softened his voice. "Maybe you could shorten the program, too. Eight weeks would be long enough, don't you think? Or even four. Situations change. You have to adjust."

With an awkward jerk, Caroline left the rocker and went to stand on the far side of the porch. "The rest of us have to adjust so you can resume your high-profile career? Is that what you're saying?"

"I'm saying I want to marry you, to live with you for the rest of our lives. I'm not trying to derail you from your work—San Francisco offers plenty of opportunities for helping kids and adults of all kinds." He crossed to stand beside her. "It's the perfect solution. Commuting would be impossible."

"I—" She crossed her arms, wrapping the blanket more securely around her, and faced away from him. Again. "I can't go."

His gut started to grind. "You'd be seeing your family just as much."

"I would be leaving all the people here who depend on me."

There was no answer he could make to that.

In an even lower voice, she said, "I'd be giving in."

"Giving in?"

"To my dad."

Ford rubbed a hand over his face. "How would marrying me mean giving in to your arrogant, overbearing, unforgiving dad? To me it seems just the opposite."

Caroline lifted her chin and, finally, turned back to meet his gaze with her own. "I don't want to be a princess anymore. I want to make a difference. In the place I call home."

"San Francisco—"

She nodded. "Sure. I appreciate that you wouldn't expect me to change my profession, as he did. Leaving Bisons Creek, though—moving to the big city to be the wife of a rich lawyer who descends from her tower to favor the less fortunate—how is that any different?"

"So you won't marry me because of my job?" Anger mixed in with the pain.

"I want to show my dad that he is wrong. That the people I work with are worth helping. I want to be their friend, a part of their lives, not separated from them by money and prestige." She put a hand on his arm. "What might have happened if we hadn't had those barriers between us in high school? We could have had a real relationship years ago."

"Maybe. I mean… That would have been—" Words failed him. Logic seemed impossible through the pain.

After a few minutes, he managed to make himself move. "You'd better get inside." He opened the door for her, but kept his distance as she walked through.

She looked at him from the threshold. Tears shone in her eyes. "I wish I could feel differently."

"I…" For a man used to thinking on his feet, he was having a lot of trouble putting ideas together. "We'll talk."

Caroline nodded and shut the door between them.

Ford went to his room and made a plane reservation for the following Sunday afternoon.

He'd said he didn't believe the kids would endure longer than two weeks at the ranch. How ironic that *he* would be the one who didn't last.

CAROLINE TRIED TO take satisfaction from the observation that the second week of ranch camp was as different from the first week as buffalo were from giraffes. Chores got done without too much complaining, even from Marcos. Mornings, the kids saddled their horses and went on long rides with her and one of the Marshall brothers while the other two got some actual ranch work done. Marcos and Thomas tried bareback riding in the corral as training for their goal of bull riding. They each fell off, more than once, but got up and on again with no complaints. Justino said he'd stick with a saddle and staying on the horse.

Nate rode Blue without a saddle and stuck to the mare like a burr, even in the field at a jog. Fortunately, the other boys mostly ignored him and didn't notice.

In the afternoons the kids worked on rodeo skills. Dylan, Garrett and Ford rigged up the bucking barrel they'd learned on themselves and started teaching Thomas, Marcos and Lena how to ride it. Caroline set up a cloverleaf of barrels on a level area in the field where Becky and Lizzie could practice racing. They started with their horses at a walk but by the end of the week, both girls were doing pretty well staying on the pattern at a jog.

Evenings became a gathering time, with the kids wanting to talk about their new skills, soaking up any tips their mentors could provide. Monday night they'd gone to the fort for a campfire, but on Tuesday and Wednesday they gathered on the front porch of the ranch house, eating homemade ice cream while they talked about horses and bulls.

Underneath the contentment, however, ran a stream of pure anguish. The awareness that Ford would be leaving hung over his brothers like a smoky haze, blurring or even hiding their usual good humor. The lines in Wyatt's face had gotten deeper overnight. Dylan's smart comments went unsaid, and Garrett's encouragement sounded forced. Caroline recognized she was failing to be as supportive, as effective with the kids as she wanted to be. Cheerful was hard to produce when your heart was broken.

And even harder when you had done the damage all by yourself.

Of them all, Ford seemed the least changed. He remained patient and positive with the kids, applauding their efforts and offering advice wherever needed. His grin appeared with about the same frequency as before, at least as far as the kids were concerned. If he didn't joke around with his brothers as much, well, they were all busy. And if he didn't share her glances, or quite meet her eyes, if there were no stolen moments of privacy for the two of them…that was wise, considering the situation. They'd been pushing their luck before. Getting caught would have been disastrous.

But she felt the withdrawal of his attention as if the sun had disappeared from the sky. A thousand times, she wanted to go to him and cancel her refusal. "Yes, I'll marry you," she would say, "and I'll live with you anywhere. I love you so much!"

Then she had to break up an argument between Thomas and Marcos over an ill-considered comment. They still had trouble with their tempers, and were always ready to take it out on each other. How could she simply abandon them to their fates?

Thursday a storm blew in, bringing heavy gray skies and a day full of rain. Ford, Dylan and Garrett worked cattle anyway, moving cows and calves from a used-up pasture to fresh grass. The kids watched television, played board games and took advantage of the chance to be lazy. Caroline figured once in two weeks wasn't too bad a record.

The wind coming off the mountains was chilly that evening, so instead of sitting on the rain-whipped porch, the teens wandered into the Marshalls' big living room, where Dylan soon had a nice fire blazing. With only a couple of lamps on, the room transformed into a warm, comfortable cave, sheltering them all from the weather. Honey moved from teenager to teenager, getting love at each stop, while Ford played the guitar and kids sang or didn't, depending on the song. Even Wyatt came out to sit with them a while and listen.

After a rousing version of "On Top of Spaghetti," Ford put his guitar in the case. Before the kids started moving, he stood up and switched on an extra lamp. Then he stood in front of the fireplace. "I have something to tell you all."

Caroline gripped her hands together. Garrett sent her a worried glance.

"I was planning to stay most of the summer," Ford said. "But my boss wants me in San Francisco, doing my job. He says show up now or I'm fired."

"That's stupid," Marcos said. "You're on vacation."

"The clients don't care about vacations. They want their work taken care of when it's convenient for them."

Lena shook her head. "You should just quit. I bet you like working here better, anyway."

Ford managed a weary smile. "That's not the issue. But I wanted to let everybody know that I'll be leaving

Sunday afternoon. I'm sorry about this—I was looking forward to what the rest of the summer holds for all of you. But you'll have a great time with Caroline, Garrett and Dylan. Maybe I can come over in August and check on your rodeo skills."

Thomas shot to his feet. "I think you're just tired of putting up with us. Two weeks is as much as you can take."

In the silence following his outburst, the screen door slapped loudly against the threshold. Caroline glanced around and realized that Nate had disappeared.

"I'm being completely honest," Ford said to Thomas. "If I don't go back, I lose my job."

"You're a lawyer," Becky said. "You can always get another job."

"There are reasons—"

"Excuses is what you mean." Justino stood and pulled Lena up beside him. "Don't bother." They went through the door. In a matter of moments all the kids left the house.

"That went well." Ford propped an elbow on the mantel and rubbed his fingers in his eyes.

Garrett got up. "You had to expect they'd be hurt. And angry." He blew out a breath. "I'll make sure they've ended up where they're supposed to."

In the corner of the sofa, Dylan stirred. "I'll come with you."

Without saying a word, Wyatt left the room, followed by Honey. Seconds later a door in the rear of the house shut with a firm thud.

Caroline eased out of the recliner. "I should check on the girls."

Ford followed her to the door. "What are you doing tomorrow morning?"

His nearness made concentrating difficult. "Um…supervising a ride in the north pasture?"

"What if we took off for a while?" One shoulder lifted in a shrug. "A few hours together before I…leave?"

"How can we do that? What excuse would there be?"

"That we're mending fences. Dylan and Garrett both hate the job, so I'll take you along instead."

"What about the kids? They're pretty smart."

"And currently furious with me. They'd probably prefer I be somewhere they aren't, anyway."

Still, she hesitated. "Dylan and Garrett won't be fooled. And Wyatt will know what we're up to."

"They're grown-ups—they'll handle it without embarrassing you. Or I'll make them sorry."

When she didn't commit, he set a hand on her shoulder. "Please, Caroline. I want to hold you when there's nobody around. I want to talk with you above a whisper. I want some time for just us."

He would be gone in a matter of days. How could she refuse? "I'd love to mend fences with you."

THEY SET OFF the next morning after breakfast in a truck instead of the traditional way, on horseback. Ford wanted to get to the fences farthest south, where the cattle had spent the spring, which would be a long day in the saddle. He didn't plan to spend that much of the day actually working.

Yesterday's rain had cleared, and the bright, warm sunshine favored their project. Caroline had never repaired fences on her dad's ranch, but she learned fast and made quick work of twisting wires together. With two people on the lookout for breaks, they covered the miles of fence line in less than two hours.

"Done," Ford declared, putting his tool bag in the bed of the truck. "We can honestly say we worked while we were out here."

Caroline frowned at him. "Do we have to go back so soon?"

"Nope. I have something to show you first. Hop in the truck."

After about fifteen minutes, they left the open pastureland of the Circle M for a more wooded area, following a small, rutted path up into the foothills of the Big Horns. Caroline cast him a couple of doubtful glances, but didn't say anything. Ford just hoped no trees had fallen to block his way.

"Okay," he said, when he could see their destination ahead, at the end of the tunnel of pines. "Close your eyes."

She obeyed but then opened one eye to peer at him again. "Don't drive off a cliff."

"I'm not closing *my* eyes."

"Just wanted to be sure."

He drove out of the shadows into sunlight and stopped the truck. "Keep 'em closed," he told her. "I'll help you out of the truck." Only when he'd lifted her down and walked her around to the front of the vehicle did he say, "Now you can look."

Caroline opened her eyes and blinked. Her jaw dropped. "Oh, Ford. How gorgeous."

The large meadow was ringed by foothills and filled with flowers. Blue spikes, yellow pinwheels and white bunches stood almost waist high, stretching from side to side under the brilliant azure of the Wyoming sky.

"I'm not sure of the names of the plants," he confessed. "I found this place one summer in high school." He cleared his throat. "My brothers have never been here."

Her smile acknowledged that gift. Turning, she studied the flowers. "Lupines are the blue ones," she said. "Balsamroot is the yellow. Lots of different whites…I can't name them all, either. Who cares? It's perfect." She spun and threw her arms around his neck, lifting her face to his. "Thank you for sharing this place with me."

"My pleasure." Indeed, the pleasure of holding her,

hard, closer than close, overwhelmed him. Her breasts firm against his chest, the softness of her belly against his hardness, the freedom to stroke her shoulders and hips and bottom… Ford held on to sanity by one slim thread.

"I have a blanket," he whispered, though he could have shouted and nobody would have heard but Caroline. "Let me…get it."

"I hate to crush the flowers," she said, when he reappeared. "Is there a bare place?"

"Over here." He led her to the edge of the trees, where the bottom branches were high but the ground underneath was relatively clear. Together they stretched the dark green blanket over the earth. Ford put the bag of food he'd brought on one corner and a cooler of drinks on another.

But having set the stage, he wondered if he'd assumed too much. He'd be leaving in two days—a planned seduction scene suddenly seemed downright dishonorable. Slam bam, thank you, ma'am, indeed.

He stood at the edge of the blanket, suddenly awkward.

Caroline glanced at him and then sat down to take off her boots, putting them on the other two corners. She knelt at the blanket's center. "Are you stalling, cowboy?"

He came down on his knees in front of her. "Maybe. I wouldn't want to take anything for granted. We don't have to—"

"Yes, we do," she said, dragging his shirttail out of his jeans. "We have to. *Now.*"

Next thing he knew, her hands slid across his skin, trailing fire where they touched. He bent to kiss her—wild, no hesitation, no second thoughts. Her tongue against his, the taste of her in his mouth—a sweetness he'd die for. She slid his shirt up to his shoulders, and he drew away long enough to jerk it over his head and off, glad he'd rolled up the sleeves hours ago.

With her face cupped in his shaking hands, Ford re-

turned for more kisses, tender this time, gentle, as she deserved. But Caroline brushed her palms across his nipples
and drove things over to the desperate side. He arched her
across his arm, swept her legs out straight and took her
down to the blanket, stretching out beside her to run his
free hand from knee to hip to shoulder before settling on
her breast.

"I love you," he said, against her lips. "I think I forgot
to say that."

She chuckled and slipped a hand under his jeans. "You
think too much."

Bare skin to bare skin, mouths fused, hands trembling,
they took and took from each other until all there was left
to do was give. Ford lay back and brought Caroline down
on top of him, watched her move, felt her body locked
around his.

Nothing in life had ever meant as much.

CAROLINE WOKE UP and realized she'd been asleep in the
open air, lying along the length of Ford's body with her
head pillowed on his shoulder.

And no clothes on, which made her smile.

"Something funny?"

She lifted her head to find him awake, too. "I haven't
run around outdoors with no clothes on since I was two
years old."

"No skinny-dipping in college?"

"Nope. You?"

"Nah. Too busy studying. I was hoping you'd made up
for it with your wild ways."

"Sorry to disappoint you."

He brought her face close to his. "The last thing in the
world I am right now is disappointed." One kiss, and they
wanted each other all over again. "See what I mean?"

"Mmm…I'm a little confused. Show me?"

She didn't fall asleep again. But as she lay there, satis-fied beyond any dream she'd ever had, the demon of re-ality snaked into her paradise. She sighed. "We should probably head home. It must be lunchtime, and I want to be there to supervise."

Ford checked his watch. "Not quite noon. But almost." Under her head, his chest rose and fell.

The spell had broken. Caroline sat up to look around for her clothes, and Ford did the same. When they'd both dressed, he put his arms around her and pulled her close. She pressed her face against his shirtfront, and they stood like that for a long, aching moment.

"Better go," he said, finally. "Lunch will be over."

Stepping away, she saw her tearstains on his shirt. "Sure."

They took the folded blanket, the cooler and the bag of untouched food to the truck. At the last moment, Caroline went to the edge of the meadow and picked a single spike of the blue lupine blossoms. To her surprise, the flowers smelled deliciously sweet, like warm honey. The fragrance filled the truck cab as Ford drove them back to the ranch.

The fragrance of goodbye.

WHILE THE OTHER kids were practicing their rodeo skills, Nate took Blue for a long ride in one of the pastures be-yond the field where the horses grazed. He didn't really know where he was going, but he figured following the fence line would bring him around to the gate eventually. The grown-ups probably wouldn't have allowed him out so far, but they tended to forget about him in the after-noons, which was great, as far as he was concerned. That was why he stayed quiet—people didn't notice if you took off to do your own thing.

He brought Blue home late in the day, about when the rodeo lessons were finishing up. Nobody had missed him, of course. Thomas and Marcos just wanted to brag about their bucking practice, Lena and Justino only talked to each other and Becky and Lizzie sat on the cabin porch with their phones. The usual routine. Funny how they'd all been so bored those first few days, and now this seemed like the only right place to be.

As he headed toward the bunkhouse, he noticed a cloud of dust on the road leading toward the ranch gate—a cloud that came in the wake of an approaching truck. Visitors weren't unusual at the Circle M, but this was a gray truck. His dad drove a gray truck.

Dread grabbed his throat as Nate waited for the confrontation he was pretty sure would be horrible.

The driver's door opened, and Travis Bradley dropped out of the seat. "Well, well, what have we here?" He slammed the door behind him. "Good to see you, boy. Wanted to come check out these fancy digs you got yourself into." He stalked up to Nate and rubbed his head, messing up his hair. "Don't believe in haircuts, I guess. You might as well be a girl."

He tucked his thumbs into the waistband of his jeans and circled around, surveying the ranch buildings. "This certainly is a fine place, ain't it? Big red barn, couple of houses, bunkhouse, corrals and fencing as far as the eye can follow. No wonder you're not at home."

The other kids hadn't noticed anything yet, but it wouldn't take long. "Mom told you where I was?"

"Hell, no. Said she wasn't sure. I had to locate my own son by asking around at the rodeo. Wasn't hard, though— everybody recognized Ford Marshall from the Circle M."

"What do you want?"

Travis grabbed his sleeve and jerked Nate closer. "Don't use that tone with me. I wanted to be sure my boy was in a decent place, that's all." He shoved Nate away. "You doing some buckin' practice?"

"Not me. I just ride."

"Of course. Why would I expect you to do something that took guts?"

The screen door on the house slapped shut. Nate glanced over at Mr. Ford, heading in their direction. "You should go, Dad. Please."

"And not say hello? What kind of manners would that be?" He stepped around Nate and waited for Mr. Ford, hands at his sides like he was ready to draw his gun. "Hey, there, Mr. Marshall. I stopped by to visit Nate."

"Welcome to the Circle M." Mr. Ford didn't offer to shake hands, as Nate had watched him do with other men. "Nate's getting along just fine with us. He's got a real talent with horses."

"Same as his daddy, if I do say so myself. I've broken my share of broncs, that's for sure."

"What else can we do for you?"

Travis nodded toward the bucking barrel. "I noticed you're doing some rodeo training with the kids. I was wondering if you could use some experienced help."

"We're good, thanks. Three of us have done roughstock events—we've got it covered."

"Well, with all these kids on your hands, you must have trouble getting the real work done. A seasoned ranch hand would be an asset. I'm glad to offer my services."

"I heard you were working for the Donnelly Ranch."

"Yeah, well, old man Donnelly and I didn't see eye to eye. I got tired of doing grunt work for that miserly bastard. I want a job cowboyin'. That's what I'm best at."

"Thanks for the offer. There are four of us, though, so we've got everything under control."

"You sure?" Travis sounded desperate. "I'm handy with cattle, fences, tractors…whatever a ranch requires, I can do it."

"I'll keep you in mind, but we're okay for now." Mr.

Ford gestured toward the gray truck. "Let me walk you to your vehicle."

Nate watched the expression on his dad's face shift to something ugly. "Throwin' me off your place? You steal my son and call it charity, but you won't give a decent, hardworking man a job?"

The other kids heard the yelling and looked over. Nate felt his face go red.

Mr. Ford stayed calm. "Don't make a scene, Mr. Bradley. Just leave."

"Oh, I'll leave." Travis marched to the truck. "But don't be surprised when everybody from here to Buffalo recognizes you for the cheap SOB you really are. Making tons of money as a fancy lawyer, but can't spare any for the ordinary folks at home." He pulled open the door and threw himself behind the wheel. "You might've fooled people before. Not now."

The gray truck reversed in a fast circle. Brakes squealed and the engine roared as Travis gunned the gas and shot down the road. If Honey had been anywhere nearby, she'd have been run over.

Mr. Ford stood with his hands on his hips, watching the truck disappear. Then he glanced at Nate. "I'm sorry I had to turn him down. But your dad's not a reliable worker."

"Yeah." Nate smoothed his hair. "I'm sorry he bothered you."

"It's okay." Mr. Ford put his hand on Nate's shoulder, but Nate braced himself not to lean into it. "We're glad to have you here, though. You're doing a great job with Blue."

"Thanks." He stepped away, and Mr. Ford let his hand fall. "I, uh, have to go cook dinner."

"Great. I'm starved." His smile seemed a little stiff, and Nate didn't believe he was happy. Mr. Ford was sad about going back to San Francisco; anybody could tell that. Being an adult evidently wasn't any easier than being a kid—at the mercy of somebody who was always angry, usually drunk and never kind.

He could predict what his dad's next move would be, of course. Fridays pretty much all ended the same way, with Travis coming in drunk at three or four in the morning, yelling to wake them all up, wanting food and company and noise to distract him from whatever bothered him at that moment. Tonight, it would be about getting rejected by the Marshalls. He'd get madder and madder until…

Nate worked with the girls to get dinner ready. He sat down at the table with everybody else, though he didn't eat much. After cleanup, everybody settled down to watch a couple of movies Mr. Dylan had brought over. Mr. Garrett and Miss Caroline made popcorn, but Mr. Ford didn't stick around. They turned out the lights to make it seem like a real movie theater, and Nate sat at the edge of the circle around the television. Little by little, he scooted farther away, until he figured he pretty much disappeared in the dark room.

When the movie action got really loud, with gunfire and explosions and craziness that had everybody laughing, he slipped out the bunkhouse door into the night outside.

And started the run for home.

Chapter Twelve

Caroline remembered very little about the movies she'd sat through, but they'd kept the kids entertained for close to four hours, and that was what counted.

"You didn't laugh much," Garrett pointed out as she washed out the popcorn bowls and pan. "Is romantic comedy more your style?"

"I'm a science fiction fan," she told him. "Give me another galaxy, and I'm glued to the screen." Tonight, though, she wouldn't have noticed if a starship had landed in the driveway. The morning with Ford was monopolizing her mind. And her heart.

"Ford likes sci-fi, too. Weird." After he dried and put away the dishes, they stepped outside into another beautiful, starry night. "So I don't suppose you were able to change his mind when you were out this morning…er…mending fences."

Heat rose in her throat and cheeks. "No. I didn't try. He's convinced he has to keep working. For the Circle M. For the family."

"I'm sorry." Garrett put an arm around her shoulders and squeezed. "There's nothing I can say to make it hurt less."

She'd started to shake her head again when the bunk-house door opened behind them. They both looked back to see Dylan standing on the threshold.

"Is Nate out here with you?"

"Not that I've noticed." Garrett wheeled around. "He's not inside with everybody else?"

"Nope."

Caroline's heart jumped with alarm. "Maybe he's in the house with Ford. Or Wyatt."

But that proved to be a futile hope. Wyatt and Ford glanced up from their work as Dylan led the way into the living room. "We're looking for Nate."

"Why would he be here?" Ford stood up. "He was at the table for dinner."

Caroline gripped her hands together. "I handed him some popcorn when the movie started."

"Where would he go?" Garrett scrubbed his face with his hands. "Why?"

"Check the barn," Ford ordered on his way to the door. "Caroline, search the cabin just in case, though he won't be there. I'll go check the pasture—maybe he's out with Blue. Wyatt, would you go through the house in case he's sneaked past us? It's stupid, but we have to cover all the bases."

They reconvened in the light from the cabin porch. "Blue's in the field," Ford reported. "But Nate is not. So the next step is to check with the kids."

They found the teenagers absorbed in their phones, or the television or each other, in the case of Lena and Justino.

"Listen up," Ford said, his voice calm but commanding. "We have a problem. Does anybody know where Nate is?"

"He helped cook dinner," Lizzie said.

"He sat beside me to eat," was Becky's contribution. "But I didn't see him actually eat much. His plate was pretty full when he got up."

Ford focused on Thomas and Marcos. "Anything?"

Thomas held his hands out, palms up. "I don't know

nothing." His attitude had gone back to resentful, the way it'd been when he arrived. "He doesn't, like, communicate."

"Marcos?"

The boy didn't meet Ford's eyes. "Nah. Haven't seen him."

"That would be the problem. Okay, thanks. Bedtime for the rest of you. Yeah, yeah," he said, over the usual protests. "Tell me about it tomorrow when you don't want to get out of the sack."

The girls reluctantly headed for the door. "I'll check in on you in a little while," Caroline promised. "Don't worry, we'll find him." She only wished she was more certain of that fact.

Thomas and Justino filed into their bedroom. Marcos simply flopped down on the couch.

Ford went to stand near the sofa. "Marcos, I need to talk to you a minute."

Marcos didn't open his eyes. "Man, I'm beat. Can't it wait till tomorrow?"

"No, it can't. Sit up." He waited until a reluctant Marcos got himself upright. Then he squatted down so they were eye to eye. "Where do you think Nate would go if he wanted to get away?"

"Why would I know?"

"That's right, you don't talk with him much. Nate's a quiet guy."

"Yeah." Marcos stared down at his hands, fidgeting in his lap. "But…well…he might've gone home. I mean, wouldn't everybody go home, if they got a chance?"

Ford didn't react. "How would he get there? Is he hitching a ride out on the road?"

"Nah, man. He's a runner, at school. He just runs into town."

Caroline gasped. "He's done this before?"

Marcos rolled his eyes and muttered a crude word. "Yeah. He went last week one night. I heard him leave, and he came in about three hours later."

She went to stand beside Ford. "And you threatened to report him if he didn't take over your chores." The boy's guilty expression confirmed her theory. "Has he gone again this week?"

"Couple of times. But he always waits till everybody's asleep. So I don't have a clue what's going on tonight."

Ford said, "Did you see his dad here this afternoon?"

"Yeah. So?"

"That's what's going on." He straightened up, started to say something…but stopped and nodded at Caroline. "Your call," he said. "I'll be outside."

She waited until he and his brothers had left the bunkhouse.

Then she turned to the boy on the sofa. "Go to bed, Marcos. But first thing tomorrow morning, pack your bags. You're going home." He protested loudly but, while she listened, Caroline didn't respond to his whines, threats or pleadings. Finally, the boy threw himself on the couch with his back to the room. End of discussion.

When she joined the Marshalls outside, Ford headed for his truck. "Garrett, let Wyatt know what's happening. Dylan, keep an eye on the boys. Caroline, you've got the girls."

"No." She spoke loudly and firmly.

He stopped in his tracks and whipped around. "No?"

"I'm going with you." He started to say something, but she held up a hand. "This is my program. My kids. And so I will be there when Nate is found."

Hands on his hips, he gazed at her. "Fine. Let's go."

"I have to check in at the cabin first. Don't leave without me."

The hint of a smile curved his mouth. "Yes, ma'am."

When she returned he was already behind the wheel of the truck with the engine idling. "Everything okay?"

Caroline buckled her seat belt. "They're in bed, but not asleep. If we don't bring Nate home soon, nobody will get any rest tonight."

They headed down the drive out of the ranch. After a couple of minutes of silence, Ford said, "You told Marcos he's going home."

"I had to. Even though it hurts me as much as him."

"You can't save everybody."

Caroline sighed. "I guess not. But I still believe everybody's worth saving."

Ford gave a rueful chuckle. "And that's why I love you, Caroline Donnelly." He reached across the console and took her hand in his. "Let's go get your lost sheep."

WHEN THEY ARRIVED at the Bradley trailer, all the lights were on, and the door hung open. The gray truck sat in the yard out front, with an old-model sedan nearby. Ford stopped his truck on the side of the road and gauged the situation.

"I don't suppose you would consider staying in the truck until I check things out?" He glanced at Caroline's set face. "I'm guessing that's a no."

"Susannah knows me. Her little girl, Amber, knows me. How scared would they be if a strange man came bursting in at one o'clock in the morning?"

The sound of breaking glass came from inside the house.

"How much more scared could they be?" Ford opened his door. "At least call the sheriff's office before you come in. I suspect we'll need some help."

"Be careful."

"You, too."

Walking across the yard, he could hear Travis Bradley

yelling. He wasn't sure what to make of the fact that no one answered. They were just scared, he hoped.

Taking the neighborly approach, he knocked on the wall beside the sagging door. "Hey, there? Anybody home?"

Travis loomed in the doorway. "What the hell are you doing here?"

"Nate went missing up at the ranch. We wanted to find out if he'd come home."

"Can't keep those kids under control? Pretty damned irrepon…irresponsible, letting him just run away." His words were slurred, his eyes glazed.

"Is Nate here?"

Bradley kicked the door open. "See for yourself."

The room was wrecked—chairs upended, dishes and glasses shattered against the walls, the television lying screen down on the floor. Susannah Bradley was huddled in a corner, holding her daughter close to her chest. The little girl's eyes were dark and round with fear. She clutched a stuffed animal just as her mother clutched her.

Ford winced as he noted the fresh black bruise around Susannah's eye, and another along the line of her jaw. This was what had brought Nate home.

The boy stood between his mother and his father, a sapling trying to stand against heavy wind. He glanced at Ford, and his cheeks flushed—he was embarrassed that Ford saw his family in this condition.

"It's okay," Ford told him. "We just want to be sure you're safe."

"Why wouldn't he be?" Travis demanded. "This is his home, not that fancy ranch of yours. I take care of my family." He reached for Nate and hauled the boy up next to him, putting a hand on his head. "Ain't that right, son?"

"S-sure."

"We don't need no inter-interference from church do-gooders and social workers. 'Specially social workers."

At that moment, Caroline came through the door.

Travis fisted his hand in Nate's hair. "Oh, great. The bitch is here, too."

Ford clenched his fists. "Watch your mouth, Bradley."

"This why you came, Miss Nosy?" He jerked Nate back and forth by the hair. "This what you're lookin' for?"

"Stop, please," Caroline said. "Let him go, and I'll leave."

"Figured you could mess with my family, didn't you? You think I'm not good enough, not man enough to take care of a wife and kids." With a shove, he sent Nate slamming into the wall. "You're just like your old man—so sure you're right and everybody else is wrong. Why, I oughta—" He grabbed Caroline by one arm, raising his fist to punch her.

In that second, Ford noosed his arm around Bradley's neck, choking him until the man's hands dropped to his sides.

With his face turning a deep red, Travis scrabbled his feet, trying to break free.

Caroline put a hand on Ford's arm. "Stop, Ford! Let him go!"

He didn't move, didn't release. After a moment, though, he shook his head and loosened the clinch. But he gave Bradley a hard shake. "You're going to behave yourself?"

"Yeah," the man whispered.

Ford thrust him away. Travis stumbled and fell to his knees, holding his throat and coughing.

"The sheriff should be here any minute," Caroline said. "Is Nate all right?"

The boy lay crumpled against the wall. Ford knelt beside him and helped him sit up. "Everything working?" he asked.

Nate managed to nod. "I'm sorry for running off," he said in his quiet voice. "But I couldn't protect them if I wasn't here." His gaze went beyond Ford. "Is he gonna be arrested?"

Sheriff's Deputy Wade Daughtry stood in the doorway, eyeing the scene. "What's going on, Ford? You causing trouble again?" Daughtry had been one of Ford's few friends in high school.

"Not me, Wade. Your culprit's over there. Mr. Responsibility."

"Right. How many times do we have to do this, Bradley? You gotta stay out of the bars, man." With no resistance from Nate's dad, he walked Travis out of the house, toward the car with the flashing blue lights.

Caroline had coaxed Susannah to sit on the sofa with Amber in her lap. Susannah had buried her face in her daughter's curly hair. Her shoulders shook with sobs.

Nate came to put his arms around his mother. "It's okay, Mom. Mr. Ford will make it right."

Deputy Daughtry reentered the house. "Are you going to press charges, Mrs. Bradley? I can get him on domestic violence, disturbing the peace, probably a dozen other violations."

Susannah looked up. "Can't you just…keep him for a while?"

"No, ma'am. Not without filing charges."

Ford squatted down in front of her. "What you should get, at the very least, is an emergency order of protection—a legal decree that your husband can't come close to you or the kids. We'll get one of those drawn up for you as soon as possible. Then we'll ask for a hearing and a permanent order to warn him off for good. You can probably keep your house, but it might be safer to go away for a few days. Do you have someone you can stay with? Family?"

She shook her head. "Nobody. Travis doesn't…make friends." As she shook her head, the tears started to flow again. "I—I don't know what to do. I don't have a job, or a place to stay... And I sound like such a loser."

"No, just a woman pushed too far. So here's what I propose." He put a hand over hers. "You and Amber and Nate can come home with us tonight. We've got room for you and Amber in the house, and Nate's got a bed he should be in." A glance at Nate got the tiniest of smiles. "I'll get the order of protection, but meanwhile you will be somewhere safe, with people taking care of you."

"I couldn't—"

"Yes, you can," Caroline assured her. "Nate can't keep running out in the middle of the night to check on you. This doesn't have to be a permanent arrangement, but you can take some time to get yourself together and figure out what you're going to do."

Nate squeezed her shoulders. "It'll be okay, Mom. You can watch me ride."

"But I can't repay you—"

Ford straightened up. "Don't worry about that right now. Just get some clothes together for you and Amber, and we'll take you to the ranch."

Still protesting, Susannah allowed Caroline to assist her in packing up Amber's clothes, plus a bag of toys. As she crossed the threshold of the front door, Nate's mother looked back into the room. "So much for a fresh start," she said. Then she closed the door behind her and walked away.

As FORD DROVE up to the ranch house, Caroline noticed a line of eerie white lights floating across the dark front porch. "What in the world are those?"

Coming closer, she answered her own question. "Oh, yes. The ever-present cell phones."

Despite the late hour, all of the teenagers had gathered on the porch. "Not one of them would stay in bed," Garrett explained as she left the truck. "They wanted to wait up till Nate came." He lowered his voice. "Though none of them would admit that, of course."

She nodded. "Of course." Turning toward the kids, she grinned. "Everything is okay, and we're all safe and sound." Physically, anyway. "So you guys should get to bed and go to sleep." The usual groans met her announcement. "Yeah, yeah. You're all night owls. But morning will be here before you know it. Nate will be along as soon as he gets his mom and sister settled. Vamoose," she said, making a shooing motion. "Git along, little doggies."

Still grumbling, the boys ambled toward the bunkhouse, except for Justino, who walked with Lena in the direction of the cabin.

Lizzie paused as she got to Caroline. "Was there a fight? Did Mr. Ford beat Nate's dad up?"

"No!" A vision of Ford's grim face as he choked Travis Bradley flashed across her mind. "It's really not your business, Lizzie. Go to bed."

The girl sighed and glanced at Becky beside her. "I always wanted to watch two guys fighting."

Becky rolled her eyes. "You're weird. Come on, I'm tired."

"I'll check on you three in a few minutes," Caroline called, mostly for Lena's benefit, since she and Justino were lingering in the shadows on the side of the cabin. "I'll expect you to be asleep."

Inside the house, she found Susannah sitting in one of the living room recliners with a mug cupped in her hands. "Hot chocolate," Garrett explained. "Can I get you a cup?"

"Sounds perfect." Something warm and sweet might dispel some of the cloud that had been hovering over her all afternoon and evening. But then she saw Ford, sitting forward in the other recliner, his elbows propped on his knees, and knew that no amount of chocolate or ice cream would cure her.

She gave a mental head shake and refocused on the matter at hand. "Did Amber settle in all right?"

Susannah smiled. "She fell asleep on the ride and never woke up. Nate's sitting with her in case she does, but I'm sure she'll sleep till morning." She pressed her lips together, glancing from Ford to Wyatt, standing in the doorway. "I can't ever thank you enough for taking us in. It's such a huge imposition, just showing up in the middle of the night."

Wyatt lifted a hand, as if to stop her. "It's not a problem at all." Caroline had never heard his voice so gentle. "I'm glad we're able to help. If there's anything else we can do, just say the word."

Nate's mother turned her face away, blinking hard.

Dylan got to his feet. "Want me to walk Nate to the bunkhouse? He's probably dead on his feet."

"Excellent idea." Ford stood up, too. "We all could probably use some sleep."

Caroline stepped forward to put a hand on Susannah's shoulder. "We'll get everything worked out. Just be confident that you and Nate and Amber are safe now."

"Thank you so much."

Ford followed as Caroline left the house. They reached the steps of the cabin at the same time as Nate and Dylan reached the bunkhouse. "Everybody where they're supposed to be," Ford commented. "Some days that's all you can ask."

Facing him from the bottom step of the porch, she gave an involuntary shiver. "That was scary, for a minute. I wasn't sure who would get hurt."

"I'm just glad it wasn't you."

She managed a small smile. "I'm beginning to wonder if you're right, after all." He waited, a question in his blue eyes. "Maybe some people just can't be saved."

Ford blew out a breath. "Maybe. But tonight it was three to one."

She gave him a puzzled look.

He took her hand. "Three people are safe who deserve it, versus the one who probably can't be changed. Pretty decent odds, if you ask me."

Across the yard, the door to the bunkhouse shut, loud in the quiet night. "Just in case," Dylan shouted.

Ford rolled his eyes.

Caroline put a hand on his chest, where his heart beat beneath her palm. "Good night," she said quietly. "Sleep well."

He touched two fingers to the curve of her cheek. "Sweet dreams."

She went into the cabin immediately, without watching him walk away. But she was certain that her dreams would be melancholy, just as she knew Ford would hardly sleep at all.

Goodbyes had that effect on people.

LATE AS IT WAS, Ford couldn't go straight to bed. Too much had happened tonight, and he was too keyed up to rest.

He wasn't the only one who couldn't settle. When he went into the house, he found his older brother in the dining room with insurance papers spread across the top of the table. Honey, of course, had no trouble sleeping and was stretched out on the floor at her master's feet. Snoring.

Wyatt glanced over as he came in. "This is a disaster."

Ford sat at the opposite end of the mess. "Leave it alone and I'll get to it tomorrow."

"Because you're the only one with brains?" Anger roughened the deep voice.

"Because I'm used to dealing with corporate crap. What is your problem?" He didn't feel so calm and collected himself.

"I'm tired of people around here treating me like an invalid. I'm not."

"You should be careful, though, if you want to still be walking when you're eighty."

"That's another thing. I don't want to be handled like I'm a frail old man. I'm not that, either."

"No, you're an ornery young man who won't listen to the doctor. Maybe the best thing I can do is leave for California and let you get on with destroying yourself."

"Maybe so."

That stung. "Really, you don't have to thank me," he said sarcastically.

Wyatt shook his head. "We're always glad to have you here. But you don't owe us anything."

"You were in trouble. What else would I do?"

"Give us a little credit. We would have managed."

"Right—with seven teenagers on top of a broken back."

"Maybe the kids wouldn't have come. I generally know my limits. But you rode to the rescue like you're the only one holding things together."

"I wanted to help."

Having gotten wound up, the boss barely heard him. "You seem to think that if it weren't for you and that job of yours, the whole damn place would fall to pieces."

"Not at all. I just want to be sure you don't have to worry about finances. Now or in the future."

"That's my job, dammit." Wyatt pushed himself to his feet and walked to the window. "Nobody asked you to go off and make lots of money. If it's what you want to do, well, okay, but we can manage one way or another. Things might not be as fancy, but the ranch will still be working and selling cattle. Dylan might have had to stay here for school, but given some of the attitudes he came home with, that might not have been such a bad thing."

"Garrett—"

"Garrett is satisfied with his church work. He doesn't need or want more than what he has."

"So if I quit tomorrow, you would all be just fine."

"Damn straight." Wyatt snorted a laugh. "Better, even, because we might get our brother here where he belongs."

Ford planted his elbows on the table and pressed the heels of his hands to his eyes. "What am I supposed to do?" He sounded like a little kid. He expected his brother to respond with an insult.

Instead, Wyatt's tone was kind. "Make your life what you want it to be, where you want it to be." He paused a few seconds. "With those you care about."

Words failed him. He didn't dare look up.

"You can't control other people. You can only make choices for yourself." After a silence, he walked close enough to put a hand on Ford's shoulder. "I'm going to bed. See you guys tomorrow."

As his footsteps retreated down the hallway, Ford dropped his hands into his lap and sat staring at nothing. He hadn't felt this confused in years—not since his dad died, and he didn't know what was going to happen to the four of them. He'd lived under a black cloud of worry for an entire decade. And he'd sworn never to experience that uncertainty again.

Today, in many ways, he faced the same dilemma. What would happen to his brothers if he left the big-money job? If he came home and built a different life?

Caroline might be willing to take the risk. His brothers, too.

But, Ford wondered, *am I?*

FORD SPENT A lot of the day Saturday in his truck. He left just after breakfast, to catch Wade Daughtry while he was still on duty. Beside him, Marcos sulked in the passenger seat.

"I'm sorry to have to take you home," Ford told the boy. "But you crossed the line once too often."

Marcos shrugged one shoulder. "Whatever."

"Do your parents know you're coming?"

"Like they care."

"Would you want to come back to the ranch?"

He caught the quick glance Marcos sent in his direction. But the mask stayed in place. "Nah. It's lame."

"Okay." Ford didn't say anything else until he pulled to a stop in front of the address Caroline had given him. "If you decide you want to try again, you could call, say after a week or so. Caroline might be persuaded to let you return to the program."

"Yeah, right." Marcos dropped out of the truck and pulled out his duffel. "I'll think about it," he said quickly before slamming the door shut and trudging toward the house. Ford made sure the boy got inside before driving off, feeling more like an executioner than an executive.

He found Wade at the sheriff's office in Bisons Creek and together they visited the Family Crisis Center in Buffalo, picking up paperwork to petition for a protection order. Back at the Circle M, they entered the house to be hit with the heavenly aroma of breakfast cooking.

Wyatt sat at the kitchen table with a full plate in front of him. Susannah turned from the stove as Ford came through the door. "What can I make you to eat?"

"I'm good, thanks. I ate with the kids. Wade, you need a working man's breakfast, don't you?"

"I'll have what he's having." The deputy sat down across from Wyatt and tucked into the plate Susannah made for him. While he ate, she went into the dining room with Ford to fill out forms.

"We'll keep visiting judges until we get one to sign an order," he promised her. "Then Wade will deliver it personally to Travis."

Susannah drew a deep breath. "Will he obey the order?"

"For his own sake, he'd better."

"Or I'll track him down," Wade said, coming in to join them. "That's a violation I don't require your permission to arrest him for."

They left Susannah cleaning up the kitchen and got into the truck, heading for the nearby ranch of Judge Raymond. "He's a good ol' boy," Wade said. "I'm expecting him to make the process quick."

But Judge Raymond wasn't home. The next three people they tried were also out of town. "Must be a judges' convention in Vegas." Ford grinned. "Wouldn't that be a sight?"

Wade shook his head. "I don't want to think about it."

During a late lunch at Kate's, they were served by the owner herself. "I hear you're turning tail and running to the coast," she said to Ford, letting his plate clatter as she set it down. "I expected better of you than that."

He winced and looked at Wade to find an expression of distress on the deputy's face. "You're leaving? Man, I had no idea."

"I have a job," Ford declared. "Remember?"

Kate frowned, and Wade shook his head. The remainder of their lunch passed in silence. They drove to the fifth judge's ranch and found him at home, but without the necessary papers to issue the restraining order. So they headed back to Buffalo, with Wade not volunteering a word on the way.

"I'll wait for the judge to get here," he said, finally, when Ford parked at the sheriff's office. "I can bring a copy out to Susannah tomorrow, once I've served the order."

"Thanks, I appreciate it." Ford was all too aware of his time ticking away. That 6:00 p.m. Sunday flight kept getting closer. He'd barely seen Caroline all day. Would it be easier to leave if he kept his distance? Or should he grab every minute to remember?

Wade stared at him through the open driver's window. "I understand you're not a criminal lawyer out in California. But we sure could use somebody honest here. I doubt it would take you long to get up to speed." He put up a hand to keep Ford from interrupting. "I'm just saying…" He pivoted on his heel and went into the sheriff's offices without so much as a wave.

Ford left the window down as he drove toward the Circle M, letting the Wyoming wind blow the cobwebs out of his brain. He hadn't slept much, and the business of the day had been a challenge. Right now he needed a clear head and a sharp focus. The next few minutes would decide the rest of his life.

He drove under the sign for the Circle M and continued along the road to the exact point where Caroline had stopped her truck that Sunday she brought him home from church. From here he could observe the rolling plains of the ranch itself, which flowed into the more rugged foothills, and above it all the Big Horn peaks still frosted white against a perfect blue sky. This was the opposite of the view he'd enjoyed on his way down through the mountains, but every bit as beautiful, every bit as stirring.

Leaning against the side of the truck, Ford took a deep, filling breath and let it out slowly. He didn't try to think, but let his brain process on its own as he watched a distant hawk drifting on air currents. Gradually, a softly spoken sentence floated into his mind.

"I couldn't protect them if I wasn't here." Nate had said that last night, talking about his mother and his sister.

That had always been Ford's goal, too—protecting his family. He'd wanted to earn enough money so they never had to worry about being poor again. He'd single-handedly tried to prove that the Marshall boys were just as good as anybody else.

But what if that wasn't what they needed anymore? Wyatt, Garrett, Dylan—they'd all made a place for themselves in the community, a name they were proud of. They didn't require or request him to defend them.

And what if the money wasn't as important as he'd believed? Maybe the help he could offer now was a different kind—the sharing of daily tasks, the shouldering of burdens small and large, the celebration of victories as they came. They'd all tried to explain that to him, in one way or another. Could be he should start listening.

He remembered being surprised that Caroline had given up her family for her job. He was the one to talk— he'd done exactly the same thing. Maybe the best gift he could offer his family was the gift of himself.

And maybe—his heart lifted as the possibility bloomed in his mind—maybe choosing to be with Caroline didn't mean abandoning his brothers. Maybe marrying Caroline was just another way to protect them—bringing a woman into the family who could share their lives, ease their worries, plain and simple make them smile. She was a genius at making a man smile.

He found himself short of breath just considering the prospect. Living on the ranch, seeing his brothers every day, holding Caroline in his arms at night…even putting up with her quixotic, bighearted ideas, like a ranch program for truculent teenagers. Legal services for battered women. *Pro bono* work for folks who couldn't afford to pay an attorney. The possibilities, as he stood there and mulled them over, were endless.

He might, indeed, end up saving the world.

Every instinct urged him to race to the house, find Caroline and drag her off somewhere private to share his new perspective. Or…forget privacy. Just propose in front of his three brothers and six crazy kids. He didn't have a ring, or a job, but she might take him, anyway.

An idea hit, and he knew instantly it was the right choice. Back in the truck, he gunned the gas, made a U-turn and headed out again. Diamonds were always nice for an engagement present.

But Ford was going for the gold.

DINNER HAD BEEN eaten and cleaned up. Caroline was sitting on the ranch house porch with Garrett and Dylan, the three of them pretending to be cheerful while they watched Justino and Thomas playing catch. The Bradley family had walked up to visit the horses. Lena, Becky and Lizzie were, predictably, focused on their phones.

At the rumble of tires on gravel, Caroline sat forward to see Ford's truck coming down the drive, towing a horse trailer.

Dylan stood up. "What's he done now?"

Garrett stayed seated. "Did we need another horse?"

The truck stopped in its usual spot in front of the house. Ford dropped to the ground on the driver's side and, without a word, headed for the trailer. The teenagers followed, gathering at the rear of the rig while he worked on the latches. Garrett glanced at Caroline as they went to join the audience. "Do you know what this is?"

"I have no idea," she said, although deep inside her heart, a tiny hope wriggled.

Ford pushed the doors open wide and pulled down the ramp. Finally, he looked at Caroline and grinned. "Why don't you unload her? She's yours." Even in the shadows of the trailer, the horse's rump glowed a rich, palomino gold.

"I—I... Oh, Ford." She walked up the ramp, touched the mare's hip and rubbed. "Hey, Allie. How are you, girl? Can you back up?" She grabbed the creamy tail and tugged gently. "Come on, Allie. That's it. Back up. Good girl. Good." The sweet quarter horse took her time but gradually, with encouragement, she came down onto solid ground. Caroline stroked the beautiful white blaze on Allie's face and felt tears running down her cheeks.

Lizzie stated the obvious. "That's the horse you rode in the barrel race."

"Is it your birthday or something?" Thomas asked.

"Or something," Ford said. "Miss Caroline knew this horse when…well, a long time ago. They make a really great pair, don't they?" He gave the lead rope to Lizzie. "You guys take her up to the corral and give her a thorough brushing. We'll keep her in a stall for a few days, introduce her to the rest of the herd gradually."

Allie walked off with her herd of caretakers. "I'll supervise," Garrett said, heading after them.

"Me, too." Dylan followed.

"Aren't they tactful?" Caroline gazed up at Ford. His face was as relaxed as she'd ever seen it. "You bought me a horse."

"She wasn't being taken care of. And that hurt you. Besides, you should have your own horse at the Circle M Ranch."

"Just for the summer? I—"

Ford took her hands in his. "How about just for the rest of your life?"

She wanted it so much, for a minute she couldn't say the words. "You're staying?" she croaked.

"If you'll have me." He kissed the knuckles of one hand and then the other. "Marry me, Caroline. You know I love you."

"Oh, yes. Yes!" She glanced at the barn. "But I can't hug and kiss you now."

"I'll take a rain check." His blue eyes glinted, and his grin was wide and free. "We've got plenty of time." He spread his arms wide. "All the time in the world."

* * * * *

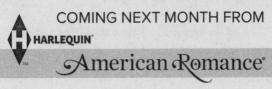
Available May 5, 2015

#1545 THE COWBOY'S HOMECOMING
Crooked Valley Ranch • by Donna Alward

Rylan Duggan finds himself off the rodeo circuit and back at Crooked Valley Ranch—too close for comfort to Kailey Brandt. She's not about to forgive him for past wrongs, but their chemistry makes him impossible to ignore!

#1546 HER COWBOY GROOM
Blue Falls, Texas • by Trish Milburn

Linnea Holland doesn't trust men anymore. But cowboy Owen Brody shows he has a kind heart beneath his bad-boy exterior and makes her think she *can* trust him—and maybe even fall in love.

#1547 THE RANCHER'S LULLABY
Glades County Cowboys • by Leigh Duncan

Ranch manager and single father Garrett Judd still blames himself for his wife's death. But bluegrass singer Lisa Rose makes embracing life too hard to resist...at least for one stormy night.

#1548 BACK TO TEXAS
Welcome to Ramblewood • by Amanda Renee

Waitress Bridgett Jameson is done being the subject of small-town gossip. Falling for handsome, mysterious ranch hand Adam Steele seems like the perfect escape from Ramblewood...until she learns his secret!

REQUEST YOUR FREE BOOKS!
2 FREE NOVELS PLUS 2 FREE GIFTS!

♦ HARLEQUIN®

American ★ Romance®

LOVE, HOME & HAPPINESS

YES! Please send me 2 FREE Harlequin® American Romance® novels and my 2 FREE gifts (gifts are worth about $10). After receiving them, if I don't wish to receive any more books, I can return the shipping statement marked "cancel." If I don't cancel, I will receive 4 brand-new novels every month and be billed just $4.74 per book in the U.S. or $5.24 per book in Canada. That's a savings of at least 14% off the cover price! It's quite a bargain! Shipping and handling is just 50¢ per book in the U.S. and 75¢ per book in Canada.* I understand that accepting the 2 free books and gifts places me under no obligation to buy anything. I can always return a shipment and cancel at any time. Even if I never buy another book, the two free books and gifts are mine to keep forever.

154/354 HDN F4YN

Name _____ (PLEASE PRINT) _____

Address _____ Apt. # _____

City _____ State/Prov. _____ Zip/Postal Code _____

Signature (if under 18, a parent or guardian must sign) _____

Mail to the **Harlequin® Reader Service:**
IN U.S.A.: P.O. Box 1867, Buffalo, NY 14240-1867
IN CANADA: P.O. Box 609, Fort Erie, Ontario L2A 5X3

Want to try two free books from another line?
Call 1-800-873-8635 or visit www.ReaderService.com.

* Terms and prices subject to change without notice. Prices do not include applicable taxes. Sales tax applicable in N.Y. Canadian residents will be charged applicable taxes. Offer not valid in Quebec. This offer is limited to one order per household. Not valid for current subscribers to Harlequin American Romance books. All orders subject to credit approval. Credit or debit balances in a customer's account(s) may be offset by any other outstanding balance owed by or to the customer. Please allow 4 to 6 weeks for delivery. Offer available while quantities last.

Your Privacy—The Harlequin® Reader Service is committed to protecting your privacy. Our Privacy Policy is available online at www.ReaderService.com or upon request from the Harlequin Reader Service.

We make a portion of our mailing list available to reputable third parties that offer products we believe may interest you. If you prefer that we not exchange your name with third parties, or if you wish to clarify or modify your communication preferences, please visit us at www.ReaderService.com/consumerschoice or write to us at Harlequin Reader Service Preference Service, P.O. Box 9062, Buffalo, NY 14269. Include your complete name and address.

HAR13R

Despite still feeling shaky, Linnea descended the steps and started walking. The day was quite warm, but she didn't care. Though she spent most of her time indoors working, there was something therapeutic about getting out in the sunshine under a wide blue sky. It almost made her believe things weren't so bad.

But they were.

She walked the length of the driveway and back. When she approached the house, Roscoe and Cletus, the Brodys' two lovable basset hounds, came ambling around the corner of the porch.

"Hey, guys," she said as she sank onto the front steps and proceeded to scratch them both under their chins. "You're just as handsome as ever."

"Why, thank you."

She jumped at the sound of Owen's voice. The dogs jumped, too, probably because she had. She glanced up to where Owen stood at the corner of the porch. "You made me scare the dogs."

"Sorry. But I was taught to thank someone when they pay me a compliment."

She shook her head. "Nice to see your ego is still intact."

"Ouch."

She laughed a little at his mock affront, something she wouldn't have thought possible that morning. She ought to thank him for that moment of reprieve, but she didn't want to focus on why she'd thought she might never laugh or even smile again.

He tapped the brim of his cowboy hat and headed toward the barn.

As he walked away, she noticed how nice he looked in those worn jeans. No wonder he didn't have trouble finding women.

Oh, hell! She was looking at Owen's butt. Owen, as in Chloe's little brother Owen. The kid who'd once waited on her and Chloe outside Chloe's room and doused them with a Super Soaker, the guy who had earned the nickname Horndog Brody.

She jerked her gaze away, suddenly wondering if she was mentally deficient. First she'd nearly married a guy who was already married. And now, little more than a day after she found out she'd nearly become an unwitting bigamist, she was ogling her best friend's brother's rear end.

Don't miss
HER COWBOY GROOM
by Trish Milburn,
available May 2015 wherever
Harlequin® American Romance®
books and ebooks are sold.

www.Harlequin.com

HARLEQUIN®

A *Romance* FOR EVERY MOOD™

JUST CAN'T GET ENOUGH?

Join our social communities
and talk to us online.

You will have access to the latest
news on upcoming titles and special
promotions, but most importantly,
you can talk to other fans about your
favorite Harlequin reads.

Harlequin.com/Community

 Facebook.com/HarlequinBooks

Twitter.com/HarlequinBooks

Pinterest.com/HarlequinBooks

THE WORLD IS BETTER WITH

Romance

Harlequin has everything from contemporary, passionate and heartwarming to suspenseful and inspirational stories.

Whatever your mood, we have a romance just for you!

Connect with us to find your next great read, special offers and more.

f /HarlequinBooks

🐦 @HarlequinBooks

www.HarlequinBlog.com

www.Harlequin.com/Newsletters

◆ HARLEQUIN®

A *Romance* FOR EVERY MOOD™

www.Harlequin.com